SUSAN SCARLETT
THE MAN IN THE DARK

SUSAN Scarlett is a pseudonym of the author Noel Streatfeild (1895-1986). She was born in Sussex, England, the second of five surviving children of William Champion Streatfeild, later the Bishop of Lewes, and Janet Venn. As a child she showed an interest in acting, and upon reaching adulthood sought a career in theatre, which she pursued for ten years, in addition to modelling. Her familiarity with the stage was the basis for many of her popular books.

Her first children's book was *Ballet Shoes* (1936), which launched a successful career writing for children. In addition to children's books and memoirs, she also wrote fiction for adults, including romantic novels under the name 'Susan Scarlett'. The twelve Susan Scarlett novels are now republished by Dean Street Press.

Noel Streatfeild was appointed an Officer of the Order of the British Empire (OBE) in 1983.

ADULT FICTION BY NOEL STREATFEILD

As Noel Streatfeild

The Whicharts (1931)

Parson's Nine (1932)

Tops and Bottoms (1933)

A Shepherdess of Sheep (1934)

It Pays to be Good (1936)

Caroline England (1937)

Luke (1939)

The Winter is Past (1940)

I Ordered a Table for Six (1942)

Myra Carroll (1944)

Saplings (1945)

Grass in Piccadilly (1947)

Mothering Sunday (1950)

Aunt Clara (1952)

Judith (1956)

The Silent Speaker (1961)

As Susan Scarlett
(All available from Dean Street Press)

Clothes-Pegs (1939)

Sally-Ann (1939)

Peter and Paul (1940)

Ten Way Street (1940)

The Man in the Dark (1940)

Babbacombe's (1941)

Under the Rainbow (1942)

Summer Pudding (1943)

Murder While You Work (1944)

Poppies for England (1948)

Pirouette (1948)

Love in a Mist (1951)

SUSAN SCARLETT

THE MAN IN THE DARK

With an introduction
by Elizabeth Crawford

DEAN STREET PRESS

A Furrowed Middlebrow Book
FM89

Published by Dean Street Press 2022

First published in 1940 by Hodder & Stoughton

Cover by DSP

ISBN 978 1 915393 16 6

www.deanstreetpress.co.uk

INTRODUCTION

WHEN reviewing *Clothes-Pegs*, Susan Scarlett's first novel, the *Nottingham Journal* (4 April 1939) praised the 'clean, clear atmosphere carefully produced by a writer who shows a rich experience in her writing and a charm which should make this first effort in the realm of the novel the forerunner of other attractive works'. Other reviewers, however, appeared alert to the fact that *Clothes-Pegs* was not the work of a tyro novelist but one whom *The Hastings & St Leonards Observer* (4 February 1939) described as 'already well-known', while explaining that this 'bright, clear, generous work', was 'her first novel of this type'. It is possible that the reviewer for this paper had some knowledge of the true identity of the author for, under her real name, Noel Streatfeild had, as the daughter of the one-time vicar of St Peter's Church in St Leonards, featured in its pages on a number of occasions.

By the time she was reincarnated as 'Susan Scarlett', Noel Streatfeild (1897-1986) had published six novels for adults and three for children, one of which had recently won the prestigious Carnegie Medal. Under her own name she continued publishing for another 40 years, while Susan Scarlett had a briefer existence, never acknowledged by her only begetter. Having found the story easy to write, Noel Streatfeild had thought little of *Ballet Shoes*, her acclaimed first novel for children, and, similarly, may have felt Susan Scarlett too facile a writer with whom to be identified. For Susan Scarlett's stories were, as the *Daily Telegraph* (24 February 1939) wrote of *Clothes-Pegs*, 'definitely unreal, delightfully impossible'. They were fairy tales, with realistic backgrounds, categorised as perfect 'reading for Black-out nights' for the 'lady of the house' (*Aberdeen Press and Journal*, 16 October 1939). As Susan Scarlett, Noel Streatfeild was able to offer daydreams to her readers, exploiting her varied experiences and interests to create, as her publisher advertised, 'light, bright, brilliant present-day romances'.

Noel Streatfeild was the second of the four surviving children of parents who had inherited upper-middle class values and expectations without, on a clergy salary, the financial means of realising them. Rebellious and extrovert, in her childhood and youth she had found many aspects of vicarage life unappealing, resenting both the restrictions thought necessary to ensure that a vicar's daughter behaved in a manner appropriate to the family's status, and the genteel impecuniousness and unworldliness that deprived her of, in particular, the finer clothes she craved. Her lack of scholarly application had unfitted her for any suitable occupation, but, after the end of the First World War, during which she spent time as a volunteer nurse and as a munition worker, she did persuade her parents to let her realise her dream of becoming an actress. Her stage career, which lasted ten years, was not totally unsuccessful but, as she was to describe on *Desert Island Discs*, it was while passing the Great Barrier Reef on her return from an Australian theatrical tour that she decided she had little future as an actress and would, instead, become a writer. A necessary sense of discipline having been instilled in her by life both in the vicarage and on the stage, she set to work and in 1931 produced *The Whicharts*, a creditable first novel.

By 1937 Noel was turning her thoughts towards Hollywood, with the hope of gaining work as a scriptwriter, and sometime that year, before setting sail for what proved to be a short, unfruitful trip, she entered, as 'Susan Scarlett', into a contract with the publishing firm of Hodder and Stoughton. The advance of £50 she received, against a novel entitled *Peter and Paul*, may even have helped finance her visit. However, the Hodder costing ledger makes clear that this novel was not delivered when expected, so that in January 1939 it was with *Clothes-Pegs* that Susan Scarlett made her debut. For both this and *Peter and Paul* (January 1940) Noel drew on her experience of occasional employment as a model in a fashion house, work for which, as she later explained, tall, thin actresses were much in demand in the 1920s.

Both *Clothes-Pegs* and *Peter and Paul* have as their settings Mayfair modiste establishments (Hanover Square and Bruton Street respectively), while the second Susan Scarlett novel, *Sally-Ann* (October 1939) is set in a beauty salon in nearby Dover Street. Noel was clearly familiar with establishments such as this, having, under her stage name 'Noelle Sonning', been photographed to advertise in *The Sphere* (22 November 1924) the skills of M. Emile of Conduit Street who had 'strongly waved and fluffed her hair to give a "bobbed" effect'. *Sally-Ann* and *Clothes-Pegs* both feature a lovely, young, lower-class 'Cinderella', who, despite living with her family in, respectively, Chelsea (the rougher part) and suburban 'Coulsden' (by which may, or may not, be meant Coulsdon in the Croydon area, south of London), meets, through her Mayfair employment, an upper-class 'Prince Charming'. The theme is varied in *Peter and Paul* for, in this case, twins Pauline and Petronella are, in the words of the reviewer in the *Birmingham Gazette* (5 February 1940), 'launched into the world with jobs in a London fashion shop after a childhood hedged, as it were, by the vicarage privet'. As we have seen, the trajectory from staid vicarage to glamorous Mayfair, with, for one twin, a further move onwards to Hollywood, was to have been the subject of Susan Scarlett's debut, but perhaps it was felt that her initial readership might more readily identify with a heroine who began the journey to a fairy-tale destiny from an address such as '110 Mercia Lane, Coulsden'.

As the privations of war began to take effect, Susan Scarlett ensured that her readers were supplied with ample and loving descriptions of the worldly goods that were becoming all but unobtainable. The novels revel in all forms of dress, from underwear, 'sheer triple ninon step-ins, cut on the cross, so that they fitted like a glove' (*Clothes-Pegs*), through daywear, 'The frock was blue. The colour of harebells. Made of some silk and wool material. It had perfect cut.' (*Peter and Paul*), to costumes, such as 'a brocaded evening coat; it was almost military in cut, with squared shoulders and a little tailored collar, very tailored at the waist, where it went in to flare out to the floor' (*Sally-Ann*), suitable to wear while dining at the Berkeley or the Ivy, establishments to which her heroines – and her readers – were introduced. Such details and the satisfying plots, in which innocent loveliness triumphs against the machinations of Society beauties, did indeed prove popular. Initial print runs of 2000 or 2500 soon sold out and reprints and cheaper editions were ordered. For instance, by the time it went out of print at the end of 1943, *Clothes-Pegs* had sold a total of 13,500 copies, providing welcome royalties for Noel and a definite profit for Hodder.

Susan Scarlett novels appeared in quick succession, particularly in the early years of the war, promoted to readers as a brand; 'You enjoyed *Clothes-Pegs*. You will love Susan Scarlett's *Sally-Ann*', ran an advertisement in the *Observer* (5 November 1939). Both *Sally-Ann* and a fourth novel, *Ten Way Street* (1940), published barely five months after *Peter and Paul*, reached a hitherto untapped audience, each being serialised daily in the *Dundee Courier*. It is thought that others of the twelve Susan Scarlett novels appeared as serials in women's magazines, but it has proved possible to identify only one, her eleventh, *Pirouette*, which appeared, lusciously illustrated, in *Woman* in January and February 1948, some months before its book publication. In this novel, trailed as 'An enthralling story – set against the glittering fairyland background of the ballet', Susan Scarlett benefited from Noel Streatfeild's knowledge of the world of dance, while giving her post-war readers a young heroine who chose a husband over a promising career. For, common to most of the Susan Scarlett novels is the fact that the central figure is, before falling into the arms of her 'Prince Charming', a worker, whether, as we have seen, a Mayfair mannequin or beauty specialist, or a children's nanny, 'trained' in *Ten Way Street*, or, as in *Under the Rainbow* (1942), the untrained minder of vicarage orphans; in *The Man in the Dark* (1941) a paid companion to a blinded motor car racer; in *Babbacombe's* (1941) a department store assistant; in *Murder While You Work* (1944) a munition worker; in *Poppies for England* (1948) a member of a concert party; or, in *Pirouette*, a ballet dancer. There are only two exceptions, the first being the heroine of *Summer Pudding* (1943) who, bombed out of the London office in which she worked, has been forced to retreat to an archetypal southern English village. The other is *Love in a Mist* (1951), the final Susan Scarlett novel, in which, with the zeitgeist returning women to hearth and home, the central character is a housewife and mother, albeit one, an American, who, prompted by a too-earnest interest in child psychology, popular in the post-war years, attempts to cure what she perceives as her four-year-old son's neuroses with the rather radical treatment of film stardom.

Between 1938 and 1951, while writing as Susan Scarlett, Noel Streatfeild also published a dozen or so novels under her own name, some for children, some for adults. This was despite having no permanent home after 1941 when her flat was bombed, and while undertaking arduous volunteer work, both as an air raid warden close to home in Mayfair, and as a provider of tea and sympathy in an impoverished area of south-east London. Susan Scarlett certainly helped with Noel's expenses over this period, garnering, for instance, an advance of £300 for *Love in a Mist*. Although there were to be no new Susan Scarlett novels, in the 1950s Hodder reissued cheap editions of *Babbacombe's*, *Pirouette*, and *Under the Rainbow*, the 60,000 copies of the latter only finally exhausted in 1959.

During the 'Susan Scarlett' years, some of the darkest of the 20th century, the adjectives applied most commonly to her novels were 'light' and 'bright'. While immersed in a Susan Scarlett novel her readers, whether book buyers or library borrowers, were able momentarily to forget their everyday cares and suspend disbelief, for as the reviewer in the *Daily Telegraph* (8 February 1941) declared, 'Miss Scarlett has a way with her; she makes us accept the most unlikely things'.

Elizabeth Crawford

CHAPTER ONE

MARDA woke up to the consciousness that she was twenty-six. There are a lot of milestones on the road of a life. There is getting into double figures, that's a fine big milestone, ten is much more important than nine. Then there are the teens, the milestone of being thirteen when you were twelve is a pretty considerable one; after that milestone talk of responsibility usually begins. Then there is the gay shining milestone for twenty-one, it is at the top of the road and a signpost by it says "freedom"; it is a lying signpost, but nobody knows that when they first reach the milestone. After twenty-one the milestones grow smaller and they shine less. The first is twenty-six. Twenty-five is still a girl, twenty-six is a woman.

Marda thought these things as she lay on her back and saw the hot blue of the July sky through the leaves of the plane tree outside her window.

"Twenty-six," she murmured, "and never been kissed except by a relation. I should think I am what is known as a failure."

She got out of bed and pulled on her dressing-gown and slippers, and went over to the dressing-table. She took up her comb, but paused with it halfway to her hair, studying her face. She gave it a nod.

"Many happy returns. You haven't improved with the years. Features irregular, grey eyes, scrubby eyelashes, and hair which, if you were honest, you would call mid-mouse."

Because she knew she was an idiot talking to her own reflection, she gave herself a shake and snatched up her washing things and went to the bathroom.

Marda was right in essentials about her appearance, but unjust to the whole. Her hair was mid-brown, her eyes grey, and her features irregular; but her eyes were full of intelligence and humour, her mouth generous, and her hair, if not distinctive in colouring, grew charmingly off her wide forehead

2 | SUSAN SCARLETT

in a natural widow's peak. She had, too, that quite undefinable attribute, personality.

Crossing to the bathroom Marda met her father, fully dressed, coming up the stairs. His face lit up at sight of her.

"Many happy returns, darling." He kissed her. "There's a parcel for you somewhere."

She gave him a hug.

"I heard the night bell. What was it? The Spooner baby?"

He nodded.

"A boy. Mrs. Spooner's all right."

She gave him a little push.

"Who would be a doctor? Go and take your things off. I won't be any time in the bath, and I'll turn it on for you." He yawned.

"I could do with a bath, and some coffee."

Marda opened the bathroom door.

"You shall have it. Lots of it, very hot and very black." Alistair Mayne had been considered brilliant in his medical student days; he had been supposed by all his friends to be certain to get to the top. He had started off as a house surgeon, and from there he had been offered two chances. One, on tuberculous research, and the other as a partner to a successful specialist. He had chosen the latter, the fact that he had fallen in love and wanted to marry influencing his choice. Two years after the marriage Marda was born, and she was followed ten years later by the twins, Edward and Clarice, and they by Timothy.

Timothy had been a frail baby, from the start a constant anxiety. Naturally Alistair called in his partner to look after his son. His partner took an infinity of trouble and endless tests and prescribed this and that, but the baby got no better. When he was one and a half he died. In the cause of science Alistair thought it his duty to find out what had been the matter with the child; his partner was away and he got an old medical school friend, who had a large general practice, to help him.

The post mortem had shown an operable condition. Appalled, Alistair had said:

"Only that, all the time."

His friend had patted his arm.

"Looks simple now that he's opened up, but mind you it's hard to detect."

"Would you have got on to it?"

The friend collected his instruments.

"Possibly, but you see I'm a G.P. I spend my days looking at sick people who've no money for expensive cures. You specialists find it hard to look for simple causes."

Alice, Alistair's wife, was up in her bedroom when he got back from the mortuary. She had a little case on the bed and was packing in it some of Timothy's things; a teddy bear, some red shoes, and a musical box. She had been crying, and her eyes were red-rimmed.

Alistair sat on the bed and told her what they had found. At the end he said:

"I dare say nobody's to blame, but I feel as if I were. I'd like to throw all this up and become a G.P. amongst quite poor people. If I did any good it would be a memorial to Timothy."

Alice looked round at their lovely house and saw quite clearly what the future would be, but her face was happy for the first time since Timothy died.

"I'd like that," she said, and went on packing.

The practice when found was a mixed one. It was in the Victoria Station neighbourhood. One part was the poorest of the poor; another, those even sadder people, starving gentility, keeping up appearances; as well, there were a sprinkling of the well-to-do. These last were known to the Mayne family as "The Jams," because they were the people who put jam on their bread. Even Hannah, the general who had been housemaid in their rich days and moved with them, knew "a Jam" when she saw one; she never had approved of Alistair ceasing to be a specialist, flying in the face of providence she called it; and when a rich patient arrived, no matter who was with him, she would burst in and whisper hoarsely in his ear, "There's a bit of Jam in the waiting-room."

Marda came out of her bath, her towel over her arm, and yelled to her father to hurry or his bath would overflow. At once the twins' doors flew open and Edward's and Clarice's tousled heads came out.

"Many happy returns, Marda."

"Good birthday, old thing."

Alice came into the passage and kissed her daughter. "Many happy returns, darling." She turned to the twins. "Hurry up, you've only ten minutes before breakfast."

"Gosh!" said Clarice. "Buck up, Edward; bet I beat you." The two doors slammed.

Marda walked to the end of the passage with her arm through her mother's.

"I'm glad the Spooner baby's arrived safely. Dad was a bit worried about her."

Alice paused at the top of the stairs.

"So am I, but—" She broke off.

Marda looked at her enquiringly.

"But what?"

Alice shook her head.

"Nothing. It's a shame to tell you gloomy things on your birthday."

Marda laughed.

"What rot! I'm not a child. I'm twenty-six, which is a woman. What is it?"

Alice's face was grave.

"Mr. French died last night."

Marda's expression altered.

"Oh no! Oh dear, bang goes the twins' school bills. I did hope he'd live till they were educated."

Alice's sense of humour, never far off, twinkled at the back of her eyes.

"Well, your father did his best to keep him going. Poor old man, he did love being alive. He died in his sleep—a lovely end."

Marda leant on the banister.

"I'm glad for him, but it's no good blinking at the fact he paid father £100 a year to go and see him every day, and what on earth are we going to do without that hundred?"

Alice shrugged her shoulders.

"Economise somewhere, I suppose."

"But where? We're down to the bone now."

Alice leant over the stairs to see Hannah was not about, and dropped her voice to a whisper.

"We could do without Hannah."

"What!" Up went Marda's chin. "Over my dead body. The house wouldn't be the same house without Hannah, she looks on it as her home."

Alice's voice was sympathetic.

"I know, darling, but we pay her forty-five pounds a year, and though that's a tenth of what she's worth, bless her, with her keep and laundry it would nearly balance the loss of the hundred pounds."

Marda's mouth was set. She turned to her room.

"No, not that. We'll have a ways and means committee after breakfast, but I can tell you here and now it's not Hannah."

The ways and means committee did not meet at all formally; it was just a gathering of the family round the table as they finished their breakfast. There were three outsiders present. "Harley Street" the cat, "Belisha" the red setter, and Hannah.

Harley Street was an accidental member of the Mayne household; he had walked in one day, a near Persian with so proud a face that he had been christened at sight.

"A cat like that," Alistair had said, "is out of place in a G.P.'s household. Let's at least show him we know he's demeaning himself by coming to us. If he's called Harley Street he'll get on to it we know where he belongs."

Belisha had been Belisha since the day, two years before, when he had been given to the family by a grateful patient. There was nothing else you could call a puppy who, although he was so small that he was apt to lurch like a drunk, was nevertheless so violent a patch of colour you couldn't fail to see him.

Hannah was in the room because she insisted on staying. She had come in with the tray to clear the breakfast things. Alice gave her a nod. "All right, Hannah, I'll give you a call. We aren't ready for a minute."

Hannah closed the door behind her and came over to the table.

"Well, I suppose I can get on with picking up the paper and string Miss Marda's presents came in."

"Not for a moment, Hannah," Alistair said. "We'll not be long."

Hannah knelt down by Marda's chair and picked up a piece of brown paper.

"I may as well be here. I've got ears in my head same as the rest of you. Wasn't it me took the message to say Mr. French was gone, poor soul. Do you think I don't know he paid you a hundred pounds a year, sir, to keep him going. Though what he wanted to stay alive for always got me; what I say is, when you can't have your pleasures you may as well get out." She gave Marda's knee a pat. "Move your chair, dear, there's a bit of string under your feet I can't get at."

Alice threw Alistair a resigned smile, then she looked down at the bow of Hannah's apron, which was all of her that showed.

"It won't interest you."

"Why won't it?" Hannah's flushed face rose over the table. "Isn't somebody going to say, 'What about Hannah?' So I thought I'd say my bit first. You can cut my wages."

Edward gave Hannah a slap on her apron bow.

"Shut up, you old fool." Marda shook her head. "We can't do that, you're practically a white slave as it is."

Clarice leant her folded arms on the table, her large blue eyes shone.

"If we've got to economise, do let me leave school. I don't believe I'll ever get my school certificate, and I'll get a job without it, honestly I will."

Her father, who was next to her, rumpled her fair curls. Clarice was slim, tall and very pretty, and he did not doubt for a moment that she would get a job without her school certificate, but he was not going to let her do it.

"No you don't, lazybones. You'll get that certificate and be trained for a job, and then you can earn your living how you like."

Marda leant back in her chair.

"Do you know, I think, Dad, you'll have to let me go."

There was a storm of protest.

"Oh darling, no," Alice implored.

"Dad couldn't do without you," said Clarice.

"There's goin' to be a nice mess-up if you aren't here, Miss Marda," Hannah objected. "I can show in the patients and put the Panels in the surgery and the Jam in here, but I can't do all that soothing-down you do when the doctor's kept."

"Besides, who's to mix the medicine?" Edward broke in.

Alistair alone seemed to consider the idea.

"I suppose you'd want a dispensary job, as that's what you're trained for?"

Marda looked at him in surprise.

"I suppose so. What else? I mean, I am a dispenser." Alistair felt in his pockets, and brought out a letter.

"I had this a couple of days ago from Ewart; he was at hospital with me. 'I suppose you don't know of a sensible woman who could take on a job needing a good deal of tact. A blind patient of mine living in Thurloe Square has suddenly inherited a ward—a girl. He doesn't feel able to tackle the job of bear-leading the child himself and frankly does not want to see much of her. He wants someone to take over most of the house, leaving him undisturbed in his own few rooms. I think he'd pay handsomely for the right person. I'm asking you to keep your eye open partly because Thurloe Square is your way, but also because I know you've got a good many new poor in your practice who might be glad of the job. Give me a ring if you can think of anybody who would do.'"

Marda leant towards her father.

"It sounds Heaven-sent."

"But what about Dad?" Edward asked again. "Who's going to mix the medicines?"

Marda got up.

"Me. If I can get the job, it'll be on condition I can have a couple of hours off each day for the surgery. Come on, Dad— ring up Dr. Ewart."

Hannah looked after Marda admiringly.

"What a girl! Always knows her own mind, Miss Marda does."

She got up off the floor, where she was still kneeling, and went for her tray.

"Though it's going to be terrible here if she gets the job. I can show the patients in, but I can't handle them."

Clarice began clearing the table.

"Cheer up. It's our holidays, and Edward and I will help you."

Hannah gave her a look.

"Thanks for nothing. I'd sooner trust to Belisha or Harley Street. Fat lot of smoothing-down you two'd do. Before we knew where we was we'd have all the patients out on the street, Jam, Panels and all the boiling."

*

Thurloe Square had that shut-faced look that London squares get in the holiday season, when in three out of every four houses the people are away. Number three hundred and one was on a corner. Marda, looking at it, thought that, though the blinds were up, it looked as shut up as the most shut house in the square. She even looked down at Doctor Ewart's card to be sure she had not made a mistake, but no, it was quite clear: "Mr. James Longford. Three hundred and one" was written on it.

"Poor Mr. Longford," thought Marda, as she climbed the steps and rang the bell. "Even if he is blind, he might have a few windows open on a day like this, and a window-box or two wouldn't hurt. I should think it would be nice when you can't see, to smell flowers."

The door was opened by a butler. A thin old yellow man, who looked as if he had been born in a cellar and never yet seen the sun. His voice when he spoke was almost a whisper. He told Marda she was expected and please to come this way.

The way led upstairs, and with every step she climbed Marda's heart sank. Used as she was to their busy clattering life at home, where anyone shouted for what they wanted, the silence of this house was uncanny. She supposed that somewhere there were servants, but if they existed they made no noise; evidently, like the butler, they had learnt to whisper, and to walk on tiptoe.

"Even if I wanted to," thought Marda, "I couldn't make a sound; this carpet's old, but it's so thick I feel as if I'd lost my feet."

The house was dreary, it had the musty smell of a museum. It had evidently been furnished in the middle of the Victorian era and apparently been untouched since. The stair curtains were heavy red satin, cracking with age. On the landing was a hideous urn filled with aspidistras, and a marble pedestal with a bust standing on it of one of the less good-looking of the Roman legionaries.

The butler opened a door at the top of the stairs and whispered: "Miss Mayne, sir," and stood aside for Marda to go in.

At all times Marda found that her emotions were apt to get a grip on her at unsuitable moments. Often in her father's surgery she had to make excuses and dash out of the room, because some little story of suffering and hardship was threatening to make her cry. Now, looking at James Longford, her eyes flooded and, since with a blind man there was no fear of being seen, they overflowed and two slid down her cheeks.

It was not so much James Longford himself that upset Marda, but the environment in which she saw him. He seemed to be a youngish man, not yet forty, she supposed. He had got up as she came in and she saw he was tall and very spare, with a beautifully cut jawbone and rather long hands. It was his sightless eyes and the hopelessly friendless look of the room that got her down.

The stairs had been depressing, but the sitting-room was ghastly. It had a wallpaper of buff with brown and yellow chrysanthemums climbing over it. The furniture was massive mahogany. There was a quite repulsive marble mantelpiece with a gilt clock on it under a glass case, flanked on either side by a gilt shepherd and shepherdess. None of the chairs looked really comfortable; the one James Longford had been sitting in Marda privately stigmatised as a perfect beast. "Anyway," she thought, "what a silly room for a blind man, cluttered up with little tables and footstools." She looked pityingly at the table by James' chair, on which was a shut Braille book. "I do believe the poor man has just been sitting doing nothing. And why on earth isn't there a wireless, and why aren't there any flowers, and what's the window doing shut up on a day like this?"

"How d'you do?" James Longford held out his hand.

Marda took it and shook it and murmured a greeting, while with the other hand she brushed away her tears.

"Oh goodness, what a dead voice," she thought. "It's as if he hardly ever talked."

James gave one of those touchingly assured gestures of the blind.

"Do sit down." He sat himself. "I think Doctor Ewart has told you what I am looking for. My great friend up at Oxford made me godfather to his child. He married before he was twenty-one; the girl is seventeen now. Her mother died when she was born. My friend died a week or two ago, and left me guardian to the girl. She's coming here."

"Poor kid," thought Marda. "What a house to come to at seventeen." Aloud she said, "When do you expect her?"

"They've been in America the last two years. He died there. She comes over on the *Queen Mary* next week. I'd want you to come in on Monday and get everything in order."

"And what you want is someone to look after her, and take her about, and all that?"

There was a pause before James answered.

"Rather more than that. I want a separate establishment run for her. There are plenty of unused rooms." He hesitated. "I lost my sight six years ago and in that time we've got into a way of living here which suits me. I don't want it upset."

Marda longed to remark, "From what I can see of your way of living it would do you good to have it changed." Instead, she said, "I see, and me, or the person like me that you will engage, is partly there to see you aren't disturbed?"

James nodded.

"That's it. Tell me something about yourself. Doctor Ewart tells me he is a friend of your father's."

"Yes, they were at hospital together. I'm a dispenser really. I trained for that directly I left school so that I could dispense for my father. But now it looks as if I'll have to take a paid job.

You see, I've got a twin brother and sister, and they're still at school, and somebody has just died who used to pay Dad quite a lot to keep him alive."

James gave a bitter laugh.

"I'd pay your father quite a lot to finish me off."

Marda decided not to notice wild talk of that kind; she went on as if she had not heard.

"I expect you want to know my age and so on. I'm just twenty-six, and I'm supposed to be capable."

"You sound just the person I need. Would you consider taking the job?"

Marda leant forward.

"Well, it depends on two things. What you would pay me, and whether I could get home every day to see to the dispensary. I don't live far from here."

He flushed slightly; evidently he did not like discussing money.

"Would you think a hundred and fifty a year fair?" Marda's eyes opened.

"It's too much. I mean, when you have to keep me."

"No, that's all right. I'm a comparatively rich man, and except for a widowed sister and her small boy I've no one dependent on me."

"And would it be all right about my going home to the surgery?"

"Do what you like. You can take my ward with you, perhaps."

Marda felt increasingly sorry for the coming girl, nobody could be less wanted.

"Of course I can," she agreed. "What's her name?"

"Shirley Kay."

"Shirley Kay," she repeated softly. "What a pretty name." She got up. "Well, as everything is settled, I'll be going. I'll be here on Monday." He got up and she put her hand in his. "Goodbye."

"Goodbye." He guided himself towards the door to open it for her. "You've a very beautiful speaking voice, Miss Mayne."

Marda was so surprised at so human a remark coming from him that she spoke in a gasp.

"Have I? Nobody ever told me that before."

He opened the door.

"Perhaps you don't meet many people who can't see. We notice voices."

"Well, goodbye," said Marda again. "I'll be here on Monday, but you won't see or hear me unless you send for me. That's right, isn't it?"

For a second it seemed as if James might be going to say, "Oh no, I'd like you to pop in now and again." Then evidently habit took possession of him: the dead dreariness came back into his voice.

"Yes, that's best," he agreed, and shut the door.

The household were on the lookout for Marda. Clarice, with Harley Street on her shoulder, was hanging out of the sitting-room window, and Edward was on the sill, holding Belisha, who looked about to throw himself into the area, by the collar. Clarice and Edward shouted as Marda came into sight.

"What luck?"

"Did he take you?"

Belisha, who hated to be out of anything, added to the noise by barking.

Hannah climbed the area steps.

"Be quiet you two, can't you." She lowered her voice and jerked her head towards the dining-room, which was also the patients' waiting-room. "Piece of Jam."

The twins at once reacted to that. Jam was Jam, and mustn't be upset by careless shouting. They retired into the sitting-room, and met Marda in the hall. Clarice pointed at the dining-room door and whispered,

"Jam."

Marda nodded and without saying a word they crept upstairs to their mother's room.

Alice was sitting by the window sewing. She turned eagerly to Marda.

"Well?"

Marda looked at Edward.

"Shut the door." She came over to her mother. "There's some Jam downstairs."

Edward was just going to shut the door when Hannah arrived.

"Leave it ajar so I can hear the bell." She fixed her eyes on Marda. "Well?"

Marda sat on the arm of her mother's chair.

"I've got it, and I can come and do the surgery. But none of you'll guess what I'm going to be paid."

"Fifty?" said Hannah.

"Fifty-two," Clarice suggested. "That would be a pound a week."

Alice's face was hopeful.

"Is it a hundred?"

Edward sat on the floor and rolled Belisha on to his back.

"Seventy-five?"

Marda shook her head.

"You're all wrong. It's a hundred and fifty. Fifty for me, and the hundred for the school bills." She hugged her mother. "Isn't it marvellous?"

"Gosh!" said Edward. "That's almost three pounds a week."

"And my keep," Marda pointed out.

Alice looked worried.

"Poor man, d'you think that being blind he's got out of touch and doesn't know what sort of salary to pay?"

Hannah sniffed.

"That's right, run her down. I call Miss Marda cheap at a hundred and fifty. To hear all of you one would think we were giving her away with a pound of tea."

Alice looked up at Marda.

"What's he like, darling?"

Marda revisioned the sitting-room in Thurloe Square, and her face was full of pity.

"I was never so sorry for anybody. He's quite nice-looking, and not old, and his blindness hasn't marred his face. But you never saw anything so friendless as his house. He's got a butler, and thick carpets, in fact everything you see in rich houses on the pictures; but if I was him I'd rather live somewhere poor and shabby, where I could hear voices and people running about. You know, Mums, going to see him was like going across the Styx. You felt as if you rowed into another world, where everybody was dead."

Hannah turned to the door.

"Sounds like you'd earn your hundred and fifty. Makes me all goose-fleshy."

Alice was concerned.

"But if it's that sort of house, what about the ward, poor child?"

"She comes from America on the *Queen Mary* next week; I'm to move to Thurloe Square on Monday. Her name's Shirley Kay, and I feel terribly sorry for her. She's only seventeen and her father's just dead, and Mr. Longford doesn't really want her, he's only taking her because it's his duty."

"Seventeen!" Alice exclaimed. "It's a shame. I must talk to your father. I think we ought to invite her here, it would be much more jolly for her."

The twins gave a whoop and rolled on the floor, roaring with laughter.

"Isn't she divine?" Clarice gurgled. "Marda goes out and gets a job because we need the money, and Mother suggests throwing away the salary and taking one extra into the family."

"Tell you what, Mum," Edward gasped when he had finished laughing. "Why don't you pay Mr. Longford a hundred and fifty as well as inviting the girl here?"

Alice shook her head at them.

"Silly children. As a matter of fact there's nothing to laugh at; we could manage somehow, and anything is better than letting a child like that go to a horrid guardian who doesn't want her."

Marda gave her mother a despairing look.

"You are such a one for jumping to conclusions. He's not horrid at all." She considered James and then added, "As a matter of fact, he's rather nice."

CHAPTER TWO

MARDA felt low-spirited as her taxi turned into Thurloe Square. Her home had seemed especially lovable when the time came to leave it. Her bedroom might be shabby, but it was so much hers, with the curtains and bedspread which had been a Christmas present, the silver cups she had won in tennis tournaments, and, above all, her especial shelf of books. Nothing makes a room so utterly yours as housing your own books.

She had a very family send-off. Edward had carried her suitcases down the stairs, singing some rigmarole he and Clarice had made up, which started, "Now our Marda's a working girl." Clarice had assisted with a musical accompaniment by tolling the dinner gong.

Alistair had come home especially to say goodbye. He had given her a hug.

"I wouldn't stand for it if we weren't going to see you every day."

Alice had laughed at herself while kissing Marda.

"Such a silly old Mums, she feels like crying; it's the idea of your not sleeping here. You've no idea how much you'll be missed, darling."

Hannah was more practical.

"Now don't forget to let me have a look at you every day when you come round. Nobody but me has ever known when you needed dosing. Of course I can't give it you last thing like I always have, but after tea will be better than nothing."

Against all this warmth the house in Thurloe Square felt like a frigidaire. The butler opening the door seemed more like a bulb growing in a cellar even than he had the other day. In a voice which sounded at its last gasp, he enquired if Marda would like to go straight to her room.

His voice, and the morgue-like quiet of the house, had a reaction on Marda. What was all this hush-hush stuff? she thought; James Longford might be blind but he was not dying, she was blessed if she was going to put up with it. In a voice which startled herself by its loudness and heartiness, she said,

"Yes, and then I'll go over Miss Kay's rooms with either you or the housekeeper."

The butler, as though watching the placing of a couple of coffins in the hall, watched the taxi-driver put down Marda's two suitcases. He waited till she had paid the man and shut the door, then he turned to her.

"There is no housekeeper, Miss."

From his voice it sounded as if the housekeeper had been strangled and her body put in the cellar; it nearly made Marda giggle.

"All right," she agreed cheerfully, "then I'll have to get you to show me. What's your name?"

"Tims, Miss." He picked up her cases. "This way, please."

It took all Marda's courage and sense of humour to bear with the rest of the day. Her bedroom and Shirley's were enough to sink any modern heart. The one allotted to her had sage-green curtains, a faded green and yellow wallpaper, and for ornament three engravings of scenes from the New Testament. Shirley's room was pink; it had evidently been designed by a woman of fluffy taste, for on every conceivable object there was a pink bow.

"My goodness," thought Marda, "I hope Shirley's the sort of girl who sees the funny side of things, otherwise she'll sit down and cry."

A large head-housemaid called Mason appeared to unpack. Marda tried to be friendly.

"Isn't it a lovely day."

"Yes, Miss."

"Makes one wish one was by the sea."

Mason raised her capped head, showing flabby pale cheeks, which had obviously not been near a beach for months.

"No, Miss. I don't care for the sea."

Marda was crushed, but she was determined not to show it.

"Perhaps you like the country better?"

Mason took Marda's best evening dress out of the case and put it on the bed. It was blue net. As she laid it down, she fingered the stuff lovingly.

"Yes, Miss," she agreed. "Maybe the country is better, but for me I like London. I was born at Deptford."

Marda had watched the affection shown her frock. She went over to the bed and picked it up.

"Is there any cupboard long enough to hang this? It's my best."

Mason's face became interested.

"Well, as for that, I don't know. I'm sure. All the furniture here is so old-fashioned." She gave a scornful nod at the mahogany wardrobe. "Nowhere to hang evening things."

"Oh dear," said Marda. "But I suppose no women ever stay here?"

"Only Mrs. Cross, Mr. Longford's sister; you know, her that has the little boy, and she only brings something in the way of an evening skirt. You see, Mr. Longford never goes out, so she sits with him."

Marda, looking round, marvelled that any woman had put up with such furnishing.

"All the same," she said, "I wonder she hasn't got Mr. Longford to get a carpenter in. It wouldn't be a big job to take that shelf out of the cupboard and raise the pegs to the top."

Mason unrolled a bottle from its paper.

"This house was left Mr. Longford by an uncle, but he never bothered with it when he could see. Then when he lost his sight he just moved in here and hadn't the heart to change anything. You can't blame him, poor gentleman, there's not much pleasure in doing a place up that you'll never get a look at."

"No."

Marda's hands arranged things on her dressing-table, but her mind was visualising James's arrival in this house. He had been blind six years, he had told her that. He would have been round about thirty then, probably had a job and, as well, a grand time with all those friends he had made at Oxford. She could imagine a modern young man sticking his nose into this place and what he would have said. She could almost hear the laugh with which he spoke about the house his uncle had left him. Probably he meant to clear it out and have it decorated, but before that his blindness came on him. She could picture those first ghastly hours when he knew his fate. He must have done what thousands would have done, gone to ground, hidden himself where no one could see him suffer; and what place could be better than this house?

"I suppose," she said, "a good many of the staff were here with Mr. Longford's uncle?"

Mason unrolled another bottle.

"All of us. You see, old Mr. Longford wasn't taken until the Christmas. Mr. Longford was abroad at the time. He came back and had a look at the place and I think he was going to try and let it, but the next thing we knew he was in a nursing home, and then as soon as he came out he came here. He hasn't been outside the door since."

Marda's eyes widened.

"Not once in six years! But what about all his friends?"

Mason shrugged her shoulders.

"They came at first, but he wouldn't see them, and after a bit they stopped coming."

"But Mrs. Cross, doesn't she get him to go out?"

Mason raised her head as if to say something, then she changed her mind.

"No, Miss."

Marda went downstairs to look at the two rooms on the ground floor which were to be sitting-room and dining-room for Shirley, and she felt almost in despair. Could she and this unknown girl exist in such an atmosphere? Then she gave herself a shake. What was the matter with her? She had two hands and a certain amount of taste; it only wanted a little contriving to make everything look quite different. She rang for Tims.

"Tims, will you go up to Mr. Longford and ask if he would see me for a few minutes."

Tims's face expressed disapproval.

"He hasn't said anything about seeing you, Miss."

Marda would have liked to have snubbed Tims, but it was obvious that, however she felt inside, she would have to keep in with the servants.

"No, he wouldn't have. But I must get his permission to get a few little things for Miss Kay. You know what young girls are."

Years before there must have been a Tims who fancied himself with the ladies. Marda's expression, 'You know what young girls are,' had been exactly right for him; it had a faintly Edwardian flavour, to which he did not exactly react but certainly inclined towards. It seemed so many years since that yellow face had smiled that it could not do it now, but it twitched where the smile might have been, and a dimly roguish look lit Tims's eyes. He hesitated for the right word, and then brought out,

"Fal-lals. All you ladies want them," and went off to James.

"Well! Well!" Marda said to herself. "We are getting on."

James, when Marda came in, was sitting just where he had been at her other interview. The room seemed even more heavy and depressing. Marda took a deep breath and raised her chin to keep her spirits up. "No good us all sinking into this lethargy," she thought.

He got up.

"So you've arrived. I hope your room is comfortable."

As he could not see her face, Marda let it express all she thought of that room.

"Yes, thank you; it wants a little something done to the cupboard if I might get a carpenter. As a matter of fact, it's about that and a few other things I wanted to see you. Can I sit down a minute?"

"Please."

She sat facing him, and felt for the words to say what she had to say, tactfully.

"There's rather a lot wants doing to the rooms for Shirley, I'm afraid."

Six years of living in the dark had evidently blunted his memory; he looked genuinely surprised.

"Is there? What's wrong?"

Marda leant forward.

"I dare say you've not been into those rooms for some time, but they are a bit depressing."

His face had the strained look of somebody seeing into the past.

"It's just as my Uncle George left it; it was furnished when he married, I suppose."

"I bet it was," thought Marda. Aloud she said, "I should think Shirley's bedroom was fixed as it is by a woman." James screwed up his face while he remembered.

"Must have been by my aunt then, Uncle George's wife, Lettice. They had a girl who died quite young, I expect it was her room."

"Well, if it was," said Marda, "I shouldn't tell Shirley, it's not likely to cheer her up."

"Of course I won't. In any case, I shan't be seeing much of her. Now, what wants doing?"

Marda counted on her fingers.

"The walls should be painted or distempered and all the paint wants doing. Curtains, chair covers, and I've not had a proper look round yet, but I expect there'll be flower vases and things wanted. Then upstairs, apart from painting and distempering, there's bedspreads and so on. I'll keep it as cheap as I can. I could make the curtains myself if I had a machine—"

He stopped her.

"There's no need for that. Ring up a good firm of decorators and order what you want. The *Queen Mary* is docking on Friday, I'm afraid you can't be ready by then."

"We can camp." She looked at him pityingly, thinking of all the fun he might have discussing the plans for doing up his house. "Are you really leaving it all to me? Don't you want to hear anything about it?"

Once more she saw that hesitation on his face, that look as if he might be going to open a window; then it died and he was a mask.

"No, you see to it. Just tell them to give you estimates and Tims can read them to me."

It was not in Marda's nature to do things alone. She was quite competent to choose the decorations for a hundred rooms, but in her mind half the fun of anything was in talking it over. The next afternoon she set off in good time for the surgery. All the family were on the lookout for her.

"Hullo."

"What's it like?"

"Do you have awfully good food?"

"Have you seen Mr. Longford again?"

Alistair put his head round his door.

"Give the poor girl a chance." He kissed her.

Marda hugged them all.

"I'll just make up the medicines, and then I'll tell you all about it. I'm having Shirley's and my rooms done up." She opened her hag and took out a collection of patterns. "Have a look through these and give me your advice, all of you."

Marda never talked when she was making up prescriptions, the horror of a mistake was always in her mind. But as she labelled the last bottle, she heard the surgery door shut on a patient, and called out to her father,

"Keep the next one waiting a second and have a word with me."

Alistair came to the door.

"Finished?" She nodded.

"Mrs. Spooner's, that's the last. How is she?"

"Fine." He put his arm round her. "I miss you not being about."

She hugged him back.

"I miss you, and all the others. That place is like a tomb. I am sorry for Mr. Longford."

"What's up with his eyes?"

"I don't know. He's only been blind six years. I suppose Doctor Ewart would know. I wish you'd find out."

Alistair raised his eyebrows.

"Why?"

Marda wriggled free of his arm and tidied the dispensary shelf.

"Not so much what's wrong with him, as if it can be good for him sitting by himself like that." She swung round to her father. "It's awful to see him. A ghastly room full of antimacassars, and he's got nothing to do, and no friends, and—"

"That sounds like his own fault. The St. Dunstan's men have proved for all time that blindness need not stop anyone from being a practically normal citizen."

Marda nodded.

"I know that, but I dare say it's easy to sort of sink into a backwood if there's nobody about to help you."

"Hasn't he anybody?"

"A sister, I believe. She doesn't sound much use. Couldn't you see Doctor Ewart?"

Alistair's eyes twinkled.

"I could, but I won't. What's the good of your having been given a fine brain and certain talents if you don't use them? You believe something could be done for your employer. Well then, it's not my job but yours to find out. You go and see Ewart."

"I don't know him."

He gave her an affectionate pat.

"Never be it said that a child of mine needed propping up. I've educated you to think clearly; well, if your thinking leads you to believe that your Mr. Longford needs help, get on with the job. It's yours."

Marda put the last bottle in place.

"All right." She grinned at him over her shoulder. "I've a good mind to answer that by saying, 'and I'll keep all I find out, and anything I can do, to myself.'"

He laughed.

"But you won't."

She kissed him.

"No, because I adore you, and you know it, you bad old man."

Marda went back to Thurloe Square warmed and heartened. She had received so much advice that she could not follow it all, but it had been fun. Clarice, whose taste was surprisingly modern for a girl who looked like the cover of a Christmas number, wanted her to go in for oiled silks. Edward had a theory that all decorations in London should be green.

"Our stinks master told me that nobody in towns looked enough at green things. He thinks people in the country have better eyes because they're always looking at grass and stuff."

"Of course, it would be fun for you to choose it all," said Alice, "but don't you think you ought to wait for Shirley?"

Marda came home with a bunch of sweet-peas. They were a present from Hannah.

"I went down to see my sister yesterday at Tring. Got a lovely show of sweet-peas. You give me a bunch of those for Miss Marda, I said. She can put them on her dressing-table and they'll make her feel more homely, poor lamb."

Because of the sweet-peas, and having enjoyed herself at home, Marda went up the stairs at Thurloe Square singing, just as she would have done if she had been at home.

"There is a lady sweet and kind,
Was never face so pleas'd my mind;
I did but see her passing by
And yet—"

As she passed James' door it opened and he came out. His face was startled.

Marda caught her breath.

"Goodness, I'm sorry. I forgot I oughtn't to sing."

James felt his way towards her.

"It's all right. I didn't mean to stop you. You left out, 'I love her till I die.'"

She laughed.

"You know it, do you?"

"Yes." He sniffed. "Don't I smell sweet-peas?"

She held them under his nose.

"Our maid at home gave them to me. They're out of her sister's garden."

He drew back his head as if something had hurt him.

"Take them away."

"Why, don't you like flowers?"

"No." He went abruptly back into his sitting-room and shut the door.

Marda stayed where she was a moment, her face quivering with pity.

"I must help him," she thought. Then she closed her eyes. "Oh God, please show me how."

CHAPTER THREE

DOCTOR Ewart lay back in his swivel chair and looked at Marda with amused eyes.

"For a doctor's daughter you are showing a lack of know-ledge of medical etiquette."

Marda nodded serenely.

"I know. But you see I want to help him, and I can't even start to do that without being unethical."

He thought a moment.

"As a matter of fact, as regards Mr. Longford's eyes, I know very little. I was not his doctor at the time of the accident."

"What sort of an accident?"

"Motor smash. He raced in those days."

"How did you come to see him, then?"

Doctor Ewart stretched out his legs, evidently preparing to talk.

"Through his sister, Mrs. Cross. I'd just brought her boy into the world. She got a chit while she was under my care from the butler to say that her brother was not well and ought to see a doctor."

Marda nodded.

"I see, that's how you came into it."

"Yes. I saw Longford. He didn't want to see me, but the butler, Tims, showed me in on him. He was suffering from a minor trouble directly attributable to his accident, which was easily cleared up."

"But his eyes?"

Doctor Ewart shook his head.

"I know nothing about them. He won't discuss his sight."

"But you've gone on seeing him?"

He smiled.

"Not professionally. I'm sorry for him. He was quite a boxer and I generally force my way in to see him after a big fight."

Marda's face lit up.

"How he must enjoy that."

Doctor Ewart shrugged his shoulders.

"I sometimes wonder. You see, he's got it into his head that if he ever showed his face all his old pals would rally round and be kind to him, and he won't take that. He said to me once that it was a bit of luck that he had that house waiting, so he could keep out of sight and be no trouble to anyone."

Marda opened both hands wide in a despairing gesture.

"But what a point of view!"

Doctor Ewart nodded.

"Shocking, but it's his, and I can't change it. Matter of fact, I've given up trying. I feel that I can do a little good by popping in now and then, but that if I say too much I may find the door shut on me. You see, he's made this isolation business a creed and a creed is a ticklish thing to handle. He considers that to keep out of the way is doing the right thing, and when a man makes up his mind what is right, it takes a change of heart to alter them."

Marda's face was horrified.

"But it isn't right. It's hopelessly wrong."

"Quite true, my dear."

"What about his sister, Mrs. Cross? Can't she persuade him?"

For the first time since the interview had started a shut-up expression appeared on the doctor's face; it was clear that discussing Mrs. Cross was a totally different proposition from discussing her brother.

"I haven't seen her for some time. The child is delicate and they live in the country." He paused and then added, rather mechanically, "Doubtless she does everything she can."

Marda lowered her eyes. "That's funny," she thought, "he doesn't like talking about her. Mason was funny about her too. I'd like to see Mrs. Cross." She got up. "I'm going to make him make an effort."

The doctor got up too.

"I wish you luck, but I doubt your getting it. Remember what I told you. Longford's idea that he should shut himself up and be a nuisance to nobody is a creed."

Up went Marda's chin.

"And my idea that God intended air to be breathed and flowers to be smelt and friends to be made is a creed, too, and it's a better creed than his, so I back it to win."

He took her hand.

"My dear child, no one can wish that more than I do. God bless you."

Out in the street the newsboys were shouting. Marda bought a paper and read it as she went along. A Portuguese ship had been caught in a typhoon and a British ship had gone to the rescue and saved the crew. It was one of those sea stories which brings a lump into the throat in the reading. That kind of shattering bravery that with a bump makes you forget that you sometimes thought civilisation not up to much.

Marda went back to Thurloe Square unconscious of the streets she passed, her eyes seeing mountainous waves and men carrying on with their life-saving in agonies of exhaustion. As she came into the house she met Tims and pushed the paper under his nose.

"Look at that. Doesn't it make you proud?"

Tims blinked and fumbled for his glasses. He read the headlines in silence. She was pleased when he looked up to see not a flush, but at least a slight touch of colour on his yellow cheeks.

"Thank you, Miss." He returned the paper. "I shall step out and buy a copy for the kitchen. It's a fine piece of reading."

Marda looked after him, her eyes laughing.

"I dare say," she told herself, "that a couple of ships full of men have almost got to drown before Tims goes to the length of stepping out and buying a paper."

Still lit up by the story of gallantry, Marda positively bounded up the stairs and, on the landing, crashed into James.

"Oh, I am sorry," she said, gripping his arm to steady him, "but I was excited by what's in the paper. Have you a minute? You must hear." Before James had a chance to protest, Marda had him back in his sitting-room and had almost pushed him into his chair and was sitting opposite to him. "Now, listen."

She read him the whole account and at the end looked up, glowing.

"Isn't that grand?" Even as she spoke, the light died out of her face. James sat in his chair as lifeless and unmoved as if she had read him the fat-stock prices. Her voice faltered: "Don't you think it's splendid?"

"Yes."

Marda felt snubbed and discouraged. She got up.

"Sorry if I've bored you. I know you like being left alone, but I thought even then you'd like to hear a story as fine as that. After all, they are our sailors." She waited: surely he would answer. But James made no move. She almost ran to the door. "Goodnight."

Outside in the passage she crumpled the paper in her hands. "He's hopeless. Absolutely hopeless. How can I help him if he won't try?" She looked down at the paper and smoothed it out; as she did so a headline caught her eye. "Tireless courage." She went up to her bedroom deep in thought. She took off her hat and stared at her face in the mirror. "Tireless courage. Everybody can have that, it's not a perquisite of sailors, and it's what you're going to need, my girl."

Burr, burr, went the alarm clock. Marda opened a sleepy eye and turned it off and sat up yawning. Half-past five! Goodness, what an hour! But today was Friday, the day for which all her planning with decorators and servants had been prepared, the day when Shirley would arrive. She got out of bed and drew back the curtains. It was fine, that was a mercy. It would be so much nicer for the poor child to arrive when the sun was shining. She was glad she had arranged to go to Covent Garden, it would make a different place of the house when it was full of flowers.

Dressed, Marda crept down the stairs and on tiptoe opened the baize door that led through to the kitchen. She was ashamed to notice her heart was beating quicker than usual.

"Goodness," she thought, "I am a fool to be scared; no one can blame me for wanting to make a cup of tea."

Marda had not yet met Mrs. Barlow, the cook; the food in the house was good, but monotonous. Sooner or later, she knew she would have to have an interview, but she was determined it should be later rather than sooner; she was nervous of cooks, women who, if interfered with, were apt to give notice.

She found the kitchen without difficulty, and there met with a shock. It was a kitchen evidently furnished with the rest of the house for Uncle George's and Aunt Lettice's honeymoon, and evidently, as with everything else, untouched since. Aunt Lettice's cook had used a kitchen range, so Mrs. Barlow used a kitchen range. There was no place where a person running out to Covent Garden at six in the morning could make a quick cup of tea.

Marda, in her annoyance, spoke out aloud.

"Dash, what a silly sort of kitchen."

She was startled by a squeak behind her, and turning, saw a wide-eyed girl of about sixteen, with her hair in curling pins and a red flannel dressing gown hugged round her.

"Hullo," said Marda, "who are you?"

The girl wriggled uneasily in her red felt slippers.

"Daisy, Miss." She jerked her head backwards. "I sleep down here. I thought you was burglars."

"What are you? A housemaid?"

"No, kitchenmaid."

"Good, then you can help me. How do I make a cup of tea without lighting that?" Marda nodded at the stove. Daisy cautiously closed the door.

"Speak low, Miss. Mr. Tims sleeps at the other end of the passage. He sleeps heavy, but he gets in a rare taking if he's woke sudden."

"Shut the door, then."

Daisy shut the door and shuffled across the kitchen.

"I'll make you a cup of tea in a jiffy, Miss, but you mustn't let on to Mrs. Barlow."

Marda laughed.

"I don't suppose she'd grudge me a cup of tea."

Daisy opened a cupboard and felt in the back of it.

"It's not that, but I have to call her at half-past seven with a cup and it's supposed to have boiled on that stove. That's how she sees I get my stove done in time; you see, it's not only for cooking, it's for the baths and that."

Daisy brought out a primus. Marda sat on the edge of the table.

"That's more sensible."

Daisy lit it.

"Mrs. Barlow doesn't like it used except when she says, but if I'm late I have to use it. I daren't take Mrs. Barlow's tea up late, proper savage she can be."

Marda watched Daisy's quick manipulation of the stove and decided that it was probably used most mornings.

"Do you like being a kitchenmaid?"

Daisy stooped to see if her flame was going well.

"No, Miss. Not so much the work, but Mrs. Barlow. But my dad said I was to stop a year, he'd take a strap to me else. Always been in good service we have."

Marda watched Daisy get out tea, sugar and milk, but when she took a tray off a shelf and began spreading a small cloth on it she stopped her.

"I don't want any of that. Just a cup at the table here. I'm going to Covent Garden to get a lot of flowers, it will cheer Miss Kay up to see flowers about."

Daisy leant against the table.

"Nice to have flowers about." Her face was wistful. "I come from the country. Mother always has a big bowl on the table, sometimes one in the window too. Got a nice little garden, Dad has."

Marda looked at her sympathetically.

"You must miss it."

Daisy turned away, swallowing hard.

"It wouldn't be so bad if I could get home of a Sunday sometimes, but it's too far. So on my Sundays I just walk about. There's not much to that when you do it alone."

Marda pulled a chair up to the table.

"Get another cup and have one with me." She watched Daisy make the tea while she turned over schemes in her mind. Daisy and her like were just the sort of people that Marda had to help. It would only need a little adjustment to see that she got home now and then, and it would make all the difference to the child.

Daisy, the tea made, sat down shyly on a chair by Marda. She gave a little giggle.

"Mrs. Barlow would come over queer if she could see us."

Marda stirred her tea.

"She wouldn't mind."

Daisy picked up her cup.

"Yes, she would. Me sitting at the table along of you, and you in her kitchen. The day after you came Mr. Tims was telling her all you were going to do to the house and she said, 'Well, she can do what she likes upstairs, but it's over my dead body she puts a foot in my kitchen.'"

Marda laughed.

"I didn't see her body as I came in, but perhaps I stepped over it."

Daisy enjoyed that joke, she would have liked to have a good hearty laugh. As she daren't have that, she held her hands to her mouth to choke back the sound.

"The things you say," she gurgled. Then as she sobered, she added: "It's going to make a lot of difference to the house having you and Miss Kay. Hear you running about and talking and that. Terrible quiet it is. There's seven of us at home, so I'm used to noise. I used to think the quiet would kill me. Still you can't wonder. I don't suppose he's got the heart to do anything, poor gentleman. It's bad he's got no relations except that Mrs. Cross and Master Edward."

Marda sipped her tea.

"Is he a nice little boy?"

Daisy made a face.

"Doesn't come here much, and when, he does I help with him on account of me being used to children." She leant over to Marda: "Needs a slipper to him if you ask me."

"He's delicate, isn't he?"

"Wouldn't be if I had him for a week. Mrs. Cross she acts silly with him, gives him everything he wants and then wonders when his stomach gets upset. He doesn't come here much, mostly she comes alone."

"Is she here often?"

Daisy nodded.

"Every month or two. If you ask me, she's coming to see how *he* is." She jerked her head in the possible direction of James. "She's got no money, he's got it all and she's watching to see nobody gets hold of any of it. She wants it all put by for Master Edward."

Marda hurriedly swallowed the rest of her tea. To have tea with Daisy was one thing, but to listen to gossip about her employer's sister was quite another. She got up, thanked Daisy and set off for Covent Garden.

Marda's arms were full of flowers, sprays of golden rod, flaming gladiolas, roses, sweet-peas. Tims's face fell as he opened the door for her. She could not stand that and at once faced him.

"Don't you like flowers?"

He shook his head.

"They're all right, Miss, but they make a terrible mess." Marda laid her armload on the hall table.

"But a worthwhile mess! Think how much nicer the house will look even if there are a few flower heads or a little pollen on the carpet. Now will you get me some newspapers and those new vases I bought."

Tims, with the expression of one arranging a funeral pyre, helped Marda spread newspapers on the table in the room she and Shirley were to use as a dining-room.

"They'll hold a terrible lot of water, these big ones," he observed sadly.

Marda was sorting out the golden rod.

"But I won't bother you with it. Just fetch me a big can and I'll get the water, and I'll have my breakfast on a tray."

It's wonderful the difference flowers can make to a house. The hall was lit by a mass of golden rod. The sitting-room was being stripped ready for decorating, but the dining-room was transformed. Masses of gladiolas flared against the sombre walls, there was a bowl of roses on the dining-table and another on the one in the window. There were two vases of sweet-peas for Shirley's room and a little one for Marda's. Even then there were some roses over. Marda held them to her face and sniffed; they smelt heavenly; they must be a pleasure to James, if only she dared take them to him. She rang for Tims; her voice was very casual.

"Tims, bring me another bowl, I have these over, they may as well go in Mr. Longford's rooms."

Tims goggled at her like a fish taken out of water.

"He wouldn't have them, Miss, he doesn't hold with flowers."

"How do you know? Have you tried putting them in his rooms?"

Tims's voice was feebler and more lacking in vitality than usual.

"No, Miss. I carry out orders. There's never been any orders about flowers."

Marda lost her temper.

"But don't you ever think of things for him? How would you like to be blind and have to think of every single thing for yourself?"

Tims was quite unmoved.

"I know my place, Miss, and I have my orders."

Marda watched his shuffling figure disappear into the servants' quarters almost stamping with rage.

"They're such a miserable lot," she stormed mentally. "How can anybody cheer up with only people like Tims and Mason about? And Mrs. Barlow sounds just as bad. The only decent person is Daisy, and I don't expect he ever meets her." She looked down again at the roses. If only she dared take them in herself, but he had been so explicit about the sweet-peas. She could still hear the tone of his voice: 'Take them away.' And her question 'Why, don't you like flowers?' and his violent 'No,' as the door shut. It was not true, of course; the warmth in his voice when he said 'Don't I smell sweet-peas?' proved that. But if you had lost your sight and were determined to shut yourself away, flowers would be a danger. There was nothing that opened the door of memory like a scent.

Staring at the roses she came to a decision. If she was to help James she must not think of herself. She must never say 'We need the money and he might give me notice.' She must never flinch from being snubbed. People who tried to push their way into other people's lives were bound to be snubbed, and, however loathsome being snubbed was, she must put up with it. Helping this man was a job worth doing and she must get on with it, and not expect any assistance. It was pretty shabby of her to have tried to have shifted her job on to Tims.

With Marda, to make up her mind was to act. She had used all the new vases, but on the mantelpiece was a marble bowl on which leant two gilt cupids.

"Pretty ghastly," she thought, "but he can't see, and it will hold water."

With the roses in their bowl, she stood outside James' door. Not only summoning up her courage to knock, but planning her campaign.

James was not sitting this time. He was over by the window. Marda took advantage of the distance his nose was from her and walked boldly across to the mantelpiece and put down the bowl and rearranged the roses.

"Excuse me bursting in, but could I have some petty cash? I spent fifteen and eightpence on flowers this morning in Covent Garden; it's a terrible lot, but it's just to welcome Shirley. I'll never spend as much again, and you did say I could get what I needed, and let you know what it cost."

James fumbled in his pocket and took out a key. He went across to his desk and unlocked a drawer and felt in the corner; he brought out a five-pound note.

"I told Tims to get this from the bank for any extras you needed. You can have any more you want, just let Tims know."

"Tims!" thought Marda, resentfully. "If only he'd say let me know,' then I'd have got a foot in as it were." She turned to the door. James felt his way after her.

"I—I hope you didn't think me rude yesterday. It was splendid what you read to me. I—I'm afraid I'm a bit of a bear these days."

Marda's smile would have done him good if he could have seen it.

"That's all right, I quite understand."

He was evidently making a great effort with himself.

"Were there—were there any further details this morning?"

She sprang on that like a cat. She had not yet seen a paper, but she was prepared to risk it; one of them was sure to have a good leader.

"Yes, lots. Wait a second and I'll get a paper and read it to you."

"Oh, no—I mean, aren't you busy?"

"Not a bit. I've been to Covent Garden. I've arranged the flowers. I'll be glad to sit down, as a matter of fact."

Marda read for an hour. There were several dangerous moments when she was turning a page and James made a movement as if to tell her to stop, but she succeeded in rattling on and never giving him a chance to break in. At the end of the hour she got up; it was clear to her that at the moment it was better she should break in and not he.

"Well, I must be going. Shirley will be here at teatime. I'll send her in to see you in the evening."

"Oh, please bring her in," said James, nervously. "I haven't seen her since she was a child. I—I've no idea what to say to her."

Marda laughed.

"I expect the right words will come to you when she's here. But I'll come too if it's any help." She sidled towards the door and turned the handle. "And if there's anything interesting in the paper tomorrow, I'll come in and read it to you." She went out and shut the door.

Outside, she waited, straining her ears. Was he coming after her to say, "No, please, I'd rather be left alone"? But there was not a sound. Marda closed her eyes: "Thank you, God, I've made a start anyway."

Marda had no preconceived ideas about Shirley. She was seventeen; she would probably be much like Clarice; she would be wearing mourning. She could not imagine further.

She tried to wait in the dining-room for the taxi to arrive, but she found herself continuously wandering out into the hall and she was there when the taxi stopped.

Her family solicitor had met Shirley, but this taxi drive she had taken alone. The first thing Marda saw was more smart luggage than she had imagined any one girl could possess. Then the driver opened the door and Shirley stepped out.

Shirley was lovely. Not the English rose prettiness of Clarice, but downright beauty. She had a little oval face and wide-apart, harebell-blue eyes, and dark hair parted in the middle, giving her the air of a twentieth-century Madonna.

"How d'you do?" said Marda, hurrying forward. "I'm Marda Mayne. I've been engaged by your guardian to see after you."

Shirley paid the taxi driver and gave orders about her luggage, then she came into the house. She smiled pathetically at Marda.

"My solicitor told me about you. It's nice you'll be here."

Marda's heart swelled with pity. Poor little thing, so lovely, and an orphan and all. She tucked her arm into Shirley's.

"Come along, you must be dying for some tea."

Shirley dropped her eyes and looked more like a Madonna than ever.

"I suppose it is teatime, but if it's all one to you I'd rather have a whisky and soda."

CHAPTER FOUR

NOTHING and nobody could utterly daunt Marda, but Shirley was a shock. Girls of seventeen in her philosophy had still one foot in the schoolroom; pretty frocks were still a novelty and gym tunics more accustomed wear. Make-up was new. When she had been seventeen she had bought a lipstick, powder and rouge, but she had used them with care, feeling slightly self-conscious. When she had been seventeen she had drunk half a glass of champagne at a wedding and felt a tremendous dog. She had been nearly eighteen before she drank her first cocktail, and then it had been especially shaken and guaranteed weak.

Shirley, sipping the whisky and soda, brought by the scandalised Tims, might as well have been Ming, the Panda, for all Marda knew of her habits. While she made vague conversation she took surreptitious glances at the girl, taking her in just as she would an animal at the Zoo.

Shirley had been two years in America and had acquired an American look and American chic. She was wearing grey; a little smartly cut grey frock with the crisp white about it beloved by Americans. She had thrown off the light grey frieze coat she had been wearing, but Marda saw that it had a scarf attached with her initials on it embroidered in black. The hat, bag and gloves Shirley had been carrying when she arrived were flung in a heap on a chair. Marda found them an impressive heap. Accessories to her at seventeen, and even now, were only accessories, and not part of each outfit. Shirley's accessories underlined her clothes. The bag repeated the initialled scarf of her coat, the gloves were an exact tone, the little hat had obviously been made to go with the outfit; there were three black bangles on her wrist with a grey ring on them.

Then her make-up was obviously no beginner's effort. Her face was tinted with a sun-warmed peach foundation, her cheeks were rouged to tone. Every eyelash was a thin bar of dark blue. Her eyelids were dimly shaded with green, her mouth flamed like a poppy. Shirley had on toeless shoes and stockings, and the toenails appearing, and her fingernails, were an exact match with her mouth. In fact, all over she was something Marda had seen on the stage, or in the picture papers, but had never supposed she would meet.

But Marda, though such polish and finish gave her an inferiority complex, was neither going to give in to it, nor to show it. She was here to look after this girl, and the fact that it was apparently years since the girl had contemplated the need for being looked after did not alter her job. For one thing she could not be sufficiently thankful, and that was her mother's advice to leave Shirley to choose the house decorations. She could have blushed to think of the amused expression there would probably have been in Shirley's eyes on contemplating her ideas of modern taste.

"Your guardian is having this room and the sitting-room next door and our bedrooms and bathroom done up," she said, hoping her voice did not sound as unnatural as it felt. "Of course I've done nothing except get a few patterns. The sitting-room is stripped so the men can start work on that right away."

Shirley looked round with a shudder.

"I'd say it needs doing up. If it wasn't for the flowers it would be pure hell."

Marda was pleased.

"I went to Covent Garden for the flowers this morning."

Shirley raised her glass.

"Here's to you, then. It was decent of you."

Marda gave a vague nod in return; she daren't say anything; she felt exactly as if she were walking on bogland and with a false step might slip through. Shirley's "it was decent of you" surprised her; it was perfectly sincere; clearly she saw that trouble had been taken and acknowledged it, but Marda felt she could also say and do the wrong thing and get an equally blunt retort.

Fortunately Shirley found her bedroom funny. She stood staring at the pink bows quite spellbound.

"Holy Mike!"

Mason, who was unpacking, looked up startled, and then remained poised over the wardrobe trunk as if she were frozen, drinking in the beauty of Shirley's clothes.

Marda sat down on the bed.

"What'll you do with it?"

Shirley looked round, consideringly.

"I think I'll have it real pretty. Flowered chintz and all those English things, you know, with one of those kidney dressing-tables kind of got up in skirts."

Mason, her arms overflowing with underclothes in crêpe de Chine and chiffon, giggled. Marda smiled.

"Oh, by the way, Shirley, this is Mason, the housemaid; she looks after us."

Shirley nodded at Mason.

"Hullo. You'll have your hands full looking after me; we had coloured help in New York, and Rosa, who saw to my clothes, said it made her feel lower than a snake to come into my room, for she surely would find something needing doing."

Marda, trying not to let her face drop at what seemed to her the entire contents of a lingerie shop, got up:

"Well, I'll leave you to wash; when you're ready I'm to take you to Mr. Longford."

Shirley took up her comb off the dressing-table.

"I haven't seen him since he was blind. He used to be a kingpin for good looks, at least that's what I thought, but I was only about ten the last time I saw him. What's he like now?"

Marda was surprised to find herself definitely minding that question. She did not want to discuss James, and she suddenly knew that she was not going to like it when Shirley, as she was sure to do, discussed him after she'd seen him. She opened the door.

"I've not seen much of him. He's still good-looking, I think. Mason will show you which my room is. Give the door a bang when you're ready."

It was three-quarters of an hour before Shirley knocked. Marda called "Come in," and then sat silent, staring.

Shirley had changed. She had on a clinging black chiffon frock and a string of pearls. She looked lovelier than ever.

"I put on this old thing," said Shirley; "it's comfortable, and I suppose Uncle Jimmie doesn't dress for dinner."

"Uncle Jimmie!"

"Yes, that's what I call him. Maybe it's a bit silly seeing he's no relation, but I always have."

"No, no, of course it isn't. It's just I'm used to thinking of him as Mr. Longford."

Shirley came over and held out her handkerchief.

"Smell, that's a new sweet-pea scent. I thought maybe he'd like to smell something good seeing he can't see anything."

"Yes," Marda agreed; her voice even to her own ears sounded dead. "Come on, I'll take you down."

On the stairs Shirley pulled Marda's sleeve.

"Say, his face isn't marked at all, is it? You see, I never knew anyone blind."

This was an angle of mind Marda could understand. She smiled reassuringly.

"No, he looks quite ordinary."

Marda was growing accustomed to James and she could see as they came in that he was nervous. He stood up as usual, but the hand which held his chair was gripped so tightly the knuckles were white.

"Is that Shirley?"

For one second Shirley faltered, then she pulled herself together and ran across the room, flung her arms round his neck, and kissed him.

"Hello, Uncle Jimmie."

James's face twitched nervously.

"Hullo, my dear." He did not exactly push her off, but he got himself clear of her arms quickly and felt his way back to his chair. "Are you there, Miss Mayne?" His voice had the anxious tone of a small boy calling out to know if Nannie is in the room.

"Yes."

A little of his tautness disappeared.

"Find Shirley a chair, will you?"

"Oh, no," Shirley protested. "I'm going to sit right here on the arm of your chair." She moved across and sat down. "I've put on my best scent just so's you should have a good smell of it." She put her handkerchief under his nose. "I'll say that's good."

James drew back his head as if he had been hit. His voice was like ice.

"I don't care for scent. Will you see Shirley has everything she wants, Miss Mayne? Goodnight."

Shirley, hurt and puzzled, stood up.

"But I say . . ."

A flood of nervous colour was rising up James' cheekbones.

"And by the way, Miss Mayne, please take away those roses off my mantelpiece. I don't care for flowers."

Shirley backed to the door, looking scared. Marda crossed to the mantelpiece and fetched the roses.

On the way she thought rapidly. This was shocking—blindness could not excuse him. Somehow she must find the words to show what she thought.

"Goodnight, Uncle Jimmie," Shirley faltered.

Marda paused by the door; her voice was resolute.

"Goodnight; I'll look after Shirley, but you have your share, you know; the poor child has been through a good deal lately and doesn't need any further suffering to add to it."

Her words hit home; the colour died out of James' face, leaving him unnaturally pale. He held out his right hand.

"Shirley, Shirley, my dear." She came back to him doubtfully and gingerly took his hand. "I—I'm afraid I'm bad company these days and best left to myself. You amuse yourself with Miss Mayne, ask for anything you want."

Outside in the passage, with James' door shut, Shirley turned to Marda, her eyes full of tears.

"Why, he's just terrible."

Shirley did not get up to breakfast the next morning, so immediately Marda had finished hers she knocked on James' door and, barely waiting for his answer, marched in and sat down; so that he could not argue about her presence, she kept up a running conversation while she opened the paper.

"Nothing much has happened today, but when we've done with the political news, there's an entertaining fourth leader on a snake which has escaped from a music hall."

Marda read for three-quarters of an hour and, as she read, she relaxed. James was not trying to stop her. She risked little pauses, and he never once broke in. When she had read all that could interest him she got up.

"Well, that's all, and I must see what's happening to Shirley."

He stopped her with a gesture.

"You thought I was unkind to her last night?"

"I didn't think, I knew you were. How would you like to have lost your father and be sent to a guardian who treated you like that?"

His fingers ran nervously up and down the groining on the arm of his chair.

"The best thing a man who, like myself, has been rendered useless, can do, is to cut people out of his life. If I start from the beginning letting Shirley see I don't want any attention, she'll know where she is. Don't want her fussing about, having some fool idea she's got to be kind."

Marda folded the paper while she considered her answer. The extreme bitterness in his voice made her feel carefully for her words.

"Shirley doesn't strike me as a person who would be kind because she thought she ought to be. I should think if she wants to be nice you might let her. She remembers you when she was ten and evidently you left a good impression."

His fingers still moved restlessly.

"When she was ten I wasn't a useless bit of waste."

If he could have seen Marda he would have noticed her body stiffen like a terrier sighting a rabbit.

"What you do with your life is your business and not mine," she said coldly, "but I don't believe anybody need be a waste unless they like it."

She thought he would turn her out on that, but instead he said, after a pause:

"There was nothing in my life as it used to be before my accident which could fit in with the existence of a blind man."

Marda could have shaken him.

"Do you suppose there was anything in the lives of all those St. Dunstan's men which fitted them to be blind?" Evidently the thought was new to him. He considered the point.

"No." He leant towards her. "I don't see why I should bother you with my point of view, but I would like you to know that I'm not suffering from self-pity."

"I never supposed you were. I think I know what you feel. You've decided that being blind you'll be a nuisance to your friends. That's it, isn't it?"

"Yes."

She clasped the paper more tightly.

"But Shirley and I don't come under that category. Shirley's only a kid and she'll like to pop in and out and tell you how things are going. I'm an employee; surely as such I can read the paper to you now and again?"

"You have. I—I can't tell you how much I enjoy it." Marda flushed with pleasure.

"And there's no reason why I shouldn't bring in a bowl of flowers now and again. It's your money that buys them."

His face was worried.

"If you were a leper, Miss Mayne, and knew you could never leave your leper island, would you deliberately hurt yourself by recalling the lands you once knew and loved?" Marda felt a longing to lay her hand on his arm.

"Yes. What's memory for if not to warm your heart in the dull, dark days."

"Dull, dark days," he repeated. He smiled. "You're a very understanding person."

"Am I sufficiently understanding to be trusted not to let Shirley and myself interfere with your life, but trusted to know when you'd like to see us and when you wouldn't?" A world of emotions dashed across his blind face, like low clouds across a sky. Marda held her breath; he looked as if he were going to say 'No.' Then the clouds passed, and with more healthy vigour in his voice than she had yet heard, he said:

"Thank you. I'll like that."

Shirley was not an easy girl to look after. While she was planning the redecoration of her rooms she was busy and contented, but that over, there seemed from her point of view nothing more to do. Two years of America, where schoolgirls are not schoolgirls as they are in England, but sophisticated people with long evening frocks, and heaps of parties lasting into the early hours of the morning, had left her expecting to be amused all day long. Yet already she was satiated with the very type of amusement she wanted. Also, though she did not know it, the hectic life she had started at fifteen had left her with stretched nerves that were easily thrown out of gear.

Marda took her to her home, hoping, very halfheartedly, that she would make friends with Clarice. It was an enterprise doomed to failure from the start. Clarice, looking the long-legged schoolgirl that she was, full of conversation made up of slang, busy with Edward from morning to night on strange amusements invented by themselves, costing no money, but immense energy, had nothing whatsoever in common with Shirley.

"Crikey!" she said to Marda, in an awed whisper after the first meeting. "She can't be only a year older than me, can she?"

Edward did not help by falling at first sight into love with Shirley. Edward had not been in love before, and his only way of expressing it was to stand staring at her with bulging eyes, or, alternatively, fetching her a whole lot of things she did not want; but if she said a word to him he turned crimson to the ears and stammered, unable to answer. Clarice took this idiotic behaviour, as she considered it, on the part of her twin, terribly to heart, but tried to disguise that she minded by making fun of the situation.

"Edward's gone goofy, he's slopping over that ghastly Shirley."

Edward could not bear Shirley lightly spoken of. "Shut up, you ass."

"I love my love with an S because she's silly," Clarice retorted.

After a few days of this Marda had a talk with Alice.

"It doesn't seem much of a success bringing Shirley here."

Alice was sitting in the window-seat darning. She looked up placidly.

"Oh, I don't know. It means you are here more, and that's good news for us."

"But she doesn't get on with Clarice, and Edward behaves like a perfect idiot."

Alice laughed.

"Dear Edward, he has 'taken well,' to speak medically, but it's not a bad thing, you know. Every boy has got to start falling in love some day."

Marda took one of Edward's socks out of her mother's basket and examined it for holes.

"I'm afraid of it spoiling their holidays. Clarice is jealous."

Alice ran her wool to and fro a moment before she answered,

"And that won't do any harm. It's time she realised she is not always going to come first in Edward's life. Besides, I think it may do her good in other ways. She asked me for a new hairbrush yesterday; she said her present one had lost half its brushing power. I didn't say that as far as that was concerned, although the brush had probably had its uses, hair brushing had not so far been one of them, but I just went out and bought her another. I shouldn't wonder if the next thing we see is Clarice taking a pride in her appearance."

Marda selected a piece of brown wool and threaded a needle.

"I'd just hate to see her growing all vain and powdered."

Alice laughed.

"She's got a long way to go before we need worry about that. If the first step is that she keeps her hair tidy and never forgets her teeth, Shirley has done quite a lot of good. Where is she now?"

"Edward's showing her his model aeroplanes, and Clarice is being rude about them."

Alice laid down her darning.

"What are you going to do with her?"

Marda shrugged her shoulders.

"Goodness knows! She's had such a good time and she doesn't like anything but buying clothes and going to cinemas, and men taking her about; and here she knows nobody. I'm wondering whether I'll send her to classes of some sort; after all, she's finishing-school age."

Alice went back to her darning.

"What sort of classes?"

"I don't know; mixed anyway, then perhaps she'll meet some people to dance with."

Alice looked startled.

"She's young to go about dancing on her own."

Marda darned rapidly.

"Not she. She's all right. She's been looking after herself in a world where the men had money to spend on drinks; she'll take a hundred students in her stride."

Marda talked to Shirley of classes that night. They were sitting over their coffee after dinner, Shirley looking lovely in a white organdie blouse and evening skirt. She had a cigarette hanging between her fingers and her head was drooped a little forward. There was such boredom in her whole attitude that Marda was touched.

"I'm afraid," she said, breaking a long silence, "you're finding all this dull."

Shirley raised her head.

"Dull! I'll say I am. But it's just as bad for you."

Marda found this an entirely new idea. Dull for her! It certainly was not. What with all she did here, and the surgery, she was busier, and now she came to think of it, happier, than she had been since she grew up.

"I'm not dull, but then, you see, I've a lot to do."

"What?"

Marda considered.

"Well, there's the flowers, and then I read to Mr. Longford, and I go to the cinemas with you, and then there's the surgery. I don't know how it is, but I don't seem to have time to be dull."

Shirley pushed back her hair with a nervous, restless gesture.

"It sounds to me just crazy. Where's the fun in all that? Don't you want to go dancing?"

Marda tapped the ash off her cigarette and thought over the question. Did she want to dance and have a good time? There was a part of the world, as she knew, that never did anything else. Did she want to be one of them? She went to a few dances, mostly at Christmas time, and sometimes to a theatre.

"I like it, of course," she admitted, "but though I expect it seems mad to you, I'm happy as I am."

"But don't you want to get married?"

Marda smiled.

"Yes—who wouldn't? But I'm not much to look at, you know. I dare say I'll never get the chance."

Shirley's brilliant eyes examined her.

"With a little money and some decent makeup, I could make you look just darling."

Marda smiled at the Americanism.

"I expect I'm better as I am. I wouldn't know what to do with myself looking 'just darling.' But I am a bit worried about you. I was wondering if you'd like to take up classes of some sort."

Shirley looked scared.

"What, go to college?"

Marda shook her head.

"No. Are you fond of doing anything? I mean dancing, or acting, or painting?"

Shirley looked interested.

"How about those art schools? I've read about them. I'd say the students have fun?"

Marda's eyes twinkled.

"But they work too. Can you paint at all?"

Shirley nodded.

"Come upstairs, I'll show you."

In the bottom of her wardrobe was a large cardboard folder and out of it Shirley took some watercolours and laid them on the bed. They were impressionistic scenes of New York. The skyscrapers on a snowy day. A waiter. A couple eating hot dogs in a drug store. Marda was amazed.

"But, my dear Shirley, these are good!"

Shirley shuffled the collection back nonchalantly into their folder.

"At school they always said I could paint."

Marda, baffled, watched the girl put the paintings back in her cupboard. That she was honestly uninterested in her own talent was clear. If she, or the twins, had a gift like that they would have been proud of it. But to Shirley all such things were of the most secondary importance. If she went to an art school and even, if once there, her work was admired, nothing to do with painting would keep her in the place; but if she found there were plenty of men and it was fun she would stop. On the other hand, who was she, Marda, to criticise Shirley's angle of mind? The great thing was that she had found a way to keep her amused. As she got up she saw a set of tennis rackets. She nodded at them.

"Are you any good?"

"Not bad."

"Would you like to play?"

"Who with?"

"Well, Clarice and Edward both play, and if Mr. Longford wouldn't mind hiring a court, I expect Edward could raise another boy to make the fourth."

Shirley closed the cupboard door and looked round eagerly.

"The seniors in a school like Edward's would be as old as me, wouldn't they? Maybe he could get one of those."

Shirley always made Marda laugh.

"Maybe he could. Are you coming down again?"

"No." Shirley shook her head. "There's no place to go, so I may as well go to bed. I've had sleep owing to me for years."

Marda kissed her.

"I shouldn't wonder if that was true. Goodnight, my dear."

Shirley gave her an unusually warm hug in return.

"Goodnight. Nice the way you worry about me. You ought to have a good time yourself, but maybe you've someone somewhere. People don't usually look like you unless there's a man about who matters."

Marda gave her a friendly slap.

"Goose! Sleep well."

Outside James' door, Marda paused, wondering whether she would go in and discuss her plans for Shirley. She never had been in after dinner; perhaps he went to bed early. On the whole she thought she would leave it till after her morning reading; she could stay on for an extra half-hour for a talk then. As she planned this she felt a lifting of her heart. She caught her breath, savouring the sensation. An extra half-hour and she was glad. What did it mean? Shirley's words came back to her. "People don't usually look like you unless there's a man about who matters." With flaming cheeks, she went thoughtfully downstairs.

CHAPTER FIVE

MARDA laid down the newspaper and looked across at James. Life for her had been an uncomplex affair. No one had crossed her path to make her heart miss a beat. She was not a person who thought of her effect on men. She treated all she had known so far just as she treated Edward. But since last night it was as if a door had opened in her mind and through it she could see something with more beauty to it than she had known there was in life. Always honest in her thinking, she knew now, looking at James, that what she would like to do would be to kneel down by him and put her arms round him and with her own warmth bring life back into him. She trembled as she thought of it and was frightened and filled with pleasure.

James had been sitting listening to the news, waiting for more. He had raised his head to ask if she had finished, but the words never shaped themselves. Emotion is like a stone dropped in a pond; a sensitive person within radius can feel it washing against them. James being blind was hypersensitive, and it was as if he was feeling an actual substance. What was this?

Marda broke the silence which was embarrassing them both. She spoke in a gabble, her words falling out on top of each other. She told him about the art school idea, and having a tennis court somewhere. She stopped because his face had puckered in the confusion of trying to follow her.

"I'm sorry, I'm talking awfully fast, but she really can paint. I think it would be a good plan."

His mind was plainly only on half of what she was saying.

"I'm sure it is."

"But of course that won't be until September, so if we could arrange about the tennis that would be something for now. I'd say, as the twins are going to come in on this, that my family would pay half, but I'm afraid we can't afford things like tennis."

He made a quick gesture.

"Please. Spend what you like, it's all right."

She got up.

"Thank you. I'll get on to that today."

"Miss Mayne," he stopped her, as she was going to the door, "is there something else?"

Marda turned, her cheeks scarlet.

"No. Why?"

He shook his head.

"I—I felt there was."

"No."

It was as if an invisible cord stretched between them; it seemed to tie Marda so that she couldn't get out of the door. Then, like fate, some street musicians, with a portable piano and three singers, began to perform in the square. At the first notes, Marda knew what they were going to sing:

"There is a lady sweet and kind,

Was never face so pleas'd my mind;

I did but see her passing by,

And yet I love her till I die!"

James got out of his chair and went to the window.

Marda held her breath. It was so long since the window had been open that it was hard to move, but he forced back the catch and threw up the lower pane.

"Her gestures, motions, and her smile,

Her wit, her voice, my heart beguile—

Beguile my heart I know not why,

And yet I love her till I die!"

James leant against the sill, the sun he had so long denied himself beating on his face. A faint wind brushed past him.

"Cupid is winged and doth range

Her country. So my heart doth change . . ."

Marda turned the door handle softly and crept out like a mother leaving a sleeping baby.

"But change the earth or change the sky,
Yet will I love her till I die!"

Outside the door, Marda stood clasping her hands. Was the window going to shut? But there was no sound. Her face radiant, she started to go upstairs and found herself face to face with Shirley.

Shirley was dressed to go out, her hat in her hand.

"You going out?" Marda said, making an obvious effort to sound natural.

Shirley leant against the banisters.

"Been enjoying the music, you two?"

Marcia struggled to make her voice light.

"Don't sing badly, do they?"

Shirley gazed at her with unabashed and calculating interest.

"It's funny now I come to think of it, but I've not dropped in to see Uncle Jimmie since I got here. Maybe he's not lost all his charm. He was a charmer, you know, when he was getting around. I think I'll look in."

Marda's hand shot out to stop her.

"Not just now. You see he's been living such an unhealthy life and this morning for the first time he's got the window wide open."

Shirley looked amused.

"Well, I shan't shut it." She gave Marda's arm an affectionate pat. "Fun's fun in this dull world; if there's any fun about let's all muscle in on it. Shan't be long." She ran down the stairs and tapped on James' door. "Can I come in?" She looked over her shoulder at Marda. "Meet you in the hall later."

James was still leaning against the window when Shirley came in. He did not seem to have heard her knock or voice. The street musicians were playing "Drink to me only with thine eyes." Shirley came across and gave him a kiss. James jumped:

"Who's that?"

She laughed.

"Shirley, of course, who else kisses you? I thought it was days I'd been in this house and not seen you, so I'd pop in and pay a friendly call."

James turned to shut the window; she put her hand on his arm.

"No, don't shut it. It's a lovely day, and I like the concert. Have you thrown them anything?"

James, felt in his pockets and produced a handful of change.

"No, you do it."

Shirley eyed the money thoughtfully and then picked out half a crown.

"I dare say you've had that much fun out of them." She leant out and waited for the end of the song, then called "Hi!" The men looked up and one held out a hat. The half-crown went spinning through the air; as it fell on the ground the man saw what it was and looked up beaming. "Thank you, Miss."

"You're worth it," Shirley called back. "Come again." James had felt his way back to his chair.

"You'll bring all the street musicians from miles around after an invitation like that."

Shirley risked a snub and sat down on the arm of his chair.

"That wouldn't be a bad thing. I'd say we could do with a little life in this square."

His voice was apologetic.

"I'm afraid it's dull for you. Miss Mayne was talking about it this morning. She's seeing what she can do about some tennis, and this art school in the autumn."

Shirley nodded.

"I know, she said she'd ask you. Tell you what I do miss, and that's a radio: maybe I could have one?"

A look of distaste crossed James's face.

"Playing jazz all day."

She leant against his shoulder.

"You have changed, Uncle Jimmie. I remember when you came that summer to Eastbourne with Daddy and me, you were just plumb crazy on orchestras."

He tried to move away from her.

"I'm older now and . . ."

She interrupted him.

"You don't look it. But you wouldn't recognise me. Do you remember how I looked then?"

He considered.

"You had two long plaits which always got wet bathing, and had to be dried by your nurse."

His voice was disinterested, but Shirley persevered.

"I'm supposed to be a bit of a glamour girl these days. I've still got that hair, of course, but now it's worn kind of parted and flat at the back. There was a paper in America said I was the best-looking brunette that ever came from England."

Shirley's complete naturalness about herself affected even James. He smiled.

"I wish I could see you."

"Must be queer," she went on, "not knowing how people look. Don't you know what Miss Mayne looks like?"

James' face was away from her and she could not see his expression, but his voice was interested in spite of himself.

"No."

Shirley's eyes twinkled.

"Well, she's one of those petite people. I think she's what they call an English rose. You know, blue eyes and yellow curls and pink and white cheeks."

James sounded surprised.

"Oh! I . . ."

"Had you thought of her differently?"

He shrank back into himself.

"I never thought about her at all."

Shirley got up; her voice took on its most wheedling note.

"Can I buy that radio? I'll keep it up in my room and you won't be disturbed a mite."

She could see he wanted her gone; that the habit of being alone, which he had taken on in the last years, made much talking exhausting to him.

"Very well. Talk to Miss Mayne about it. She'll see you get what you want."

Shirley gave him a light kiss.

"Thank you, Uncle Jimmie. Goodbye."

Marda was in the hall as Shirley came bounding down. She was determined not to cross-examine her about, her talk with James, but Shirley needed no cross-questioning. She seized Marda's arm.

"Come on. We're going shopping. We're buying a radio."

Marda's feelings were mixed. She wished she had been the one to persuade James to buy it, but she was glad he was going to have one.

"Oh, I am glad. It'll do him such a lot of good."

Shirley made a face.

"I've not made him see that much sense. I had to promise I'd keep it where he wouldn't hear it. But I'd take a bet we'll have him listening to it before long." She giggled. "I'll tell you something to make you laugh. We got talking about how I looked, and I said, wasn't he interested to know how you looked?"

"I'm sure he wasn't," said Marda, quickly.

"Well, I wouldn't say he was exactly interested in anything," Shirley agreed, "but I would say he showed a mite of interest in that."

"Pity you hadn't something more attractive to describe," Marda retorted, dryly.

Shirley giggled.

"That's where the laugh comes. I dolled you up so your own mother wouldn't know you. I said you were an English rose, golden curls, pink and white, blue eyes, and all."

Marda stopped walking, her face horrified.

"Whatever did you say that for?"

Shirley was quite composed.

"Well, I like how you look and I guess I could make something of you, but you're kind of homely when you're just described and not seen."

"But you lied."

"Well, he'll never know. I thought it was a bit of fun for him to think he had two knockouts around. Besides, I thought I'd keep our types apart. A man either falls for brunettes, or he likes blondes, or it's a redhead, but one thing is sure, he likes a type; and if you aren't his type, you can chew off the bedpost but you won't get him."

Marda felt beaten.

"I don't know what to say to you."

Shirley continued placidly with her train of thought.

"Of course, really you're half-way, neither a blonde nor a brunette, and I've made you a full blonde. It's a gamble: if blondes are his money it's your day."

Marda took hold of Shirley by the arm and gave her a little shake; she was half laughing and half furious.

"You are the most horrible child. Do you ever think of anything else except men, and how they react to you?"

Shirley raised her head. Her hat was still in her hand, and the sun, burnishing her hair, gave her more than ever the look of a Lenci Madonna. Her eyes were surprised.

"I'd say I don't. What else is there to think about?"

That evening Shirley decided to play with her new wireless, so Marda went home alone, and she was glad. She was used to her life going its unruffled way, and since the morning she had felt emotionally disturbed. She liked to feel in perfect order mentally and physically, and today, mentally, she was confused. James was her employer, and he was blind and she was sorry for him, but somehow her feelings about him did not end there. She found herself thinking about him almost all the time, and when she was with him she wanted to touch him, and even when she was not with him her mind got out of control and she dreamed, only for a second at a time, but still she dreamed, that she was not just reading the paper to him, but holding his hand, and as the dream recurred she felt tremors of pleasure run through her. To Marda there was something silly, if not unwholesome, in what she called to herself her sloppiness. She partly blamed Shirley. It was difficult to be with the girl much without considering all men as Men with a capital M, and not merely, as she had done previously, as friends of the opposite sex.

"It will do me good to get a breath of home air," she thought. "There's something queer about that house. Home's like a cold bath after a warm scented one, and it's a cold bath I need."

Home was looking satisfactorily itself that afternoon. Alice was sitting sewing by the open drawing-room window, with Harley Street lying on the window ledge beside her.

Hannah was watering some rather sad-looking parsley she kept in pots on the kitchen window ledge. She looked up beaming at Marda.

"How are you, dear?"

Marda leant over the area railings.

"Grand. How's the crops?"

Hannah shook her head.

"Not up to much. They don't get the rain on them like they ought, because I have to keep the pots on the sill. If I put them on the ground it's not only Belisha who's familiar with them, but every dog for miles around is down here making use of them, and it puts you off the parsley."

Marda laughed and ran up the steps into the house. Alice laid down her work as she came in.

"How are you getting on? Got a minute to spare, or have you got to go straight to your dispensary?"

Marda pulled off her hat and sat on the floor at her mother's feet, and rested her back against her knees.

"Not for a minute. Where are the twins?"

"On the Inner Circle. They've invented some game of hide and seek. One gets a start of five minutes and then the other goes after them. The hare can never stay in any train longer than two stations. The hound has Belisha with him, which probably slows him up as he gets so tangled upon a lead," she sighed. "It's wonderful what cheap amusements they invent. I wish I could give them more fun."

Marda rested an arm on Alice's knee.

"They're going to get some tennis. Mr. Longford will hire a court or make them members of a club. Shirley's at such a loose end. Do you suppose Edward can lay hands on a fourth? Shirley wants a senior boy; she doesn't like them too young."

Alice laughed.

"Edward would do anything for Shirley, but I think he's going to find it a bit of a struggle to go out and look for Don Juans for her, he's trying so hard to be one himself." She picked up her sewing. "It's good of Mr. Longford to arrange the tennis. I quite see it's for Shirley but it'll be very nice for the children." Alice stopped working for a moment and looked at her daughter's face. "Is something worrying you?"

Marda shook her head.

"No, I get out of sorts in that house. It isn't me. Shirley thinks nothing matters but men, and the effect you're making on them. I like men, but I like them as friends. To hear Shirley you would think you couldn't be friends with a man."

Marda was looking at the floor and Alice smiled down at the top of her head.

"You're both right. Shirley's a puss and will spend her life leading men up and down garden paths; and you will be so afraid of sentiment that perhaps you won't recognise love when you see it. The man you marry has to be more than a friend, remember; he has to be a lover, too."

Marda flushed.

"Oh, marry!" she said in an embarrassed voice, and scrambled to her feet. "One can't look at every man as though one were going to marry him."

"No," Alice agreed placidly. "Nor need one go through life treating every man as though he had come to mend the telephone; for one man is going to be very important."

Marda's cheeks were burning. She kept her head away from her mother.

"You're worse than Shirley."

In the dispensary Marda let out her sense of discomfort with the world by making an unnecessary fuss. She slammed open a cupboard, set out her medicine bottles with a clatter, and turned on the hot-water tap at full blast. Alistair put his head round.

"Hullo, daughter, you sound as if you were having what we used to call in the hospital a righteous clean-up. The nurses were always having them when they felt they had been ill-used. Has anyone been ill-using you?"

Marda turned off the tap and came over and kissed her father.

"No. But I am having a righteous clean-up. I feel black-doggish."

"Did it just come on you? Or was there any reason?"

She straightened his tie, and made a face.

"Do you ever get moments when you wish you hadn't grown up?"

He smiled rather sadly.

"Often. Those days when making ends meet wasn't my responsibility. When one woke up in the morning without a care in the world."

"And things were always the same; you just took them as they came, and didn't have to feel more than you wanted to."

He held her by the elbows.

"Why this nostalgic talk? Who's making you feel something you don't want to?"

She pulled away from him.

"Nobody. I don't know what I do mean. I expect what I need is some good hard work. I'll go and make up the medicines."

He looked after her with loving amusement.

"I expect your trouble is that you're growing up. It always hurts."

Tims came into the kitchen where the maids were already at tea. He sat down in his place with the air of a man full of momentous tidings. Mrs. Barlow lifted the teapot.

"Out with it, Mr. Tims. I can see you have something on your mind."

Tims helped himself to bread and butter.

"Seems hardly possible now that it's only seven weeks back that I returned from my holiday, and I said to you, Mrs. Barlow, 'Everything going on as usual?' and you said, 'You can be sure of that, Mr. Tims, even with you away and that temporary man in your place, everything's gone on just the same.'"

Mason passed him his cup of tea.

"What's happened?"

Tims stirred his tea before he answered.

"You know that wireless set Miss Shirley bought ten days ago, and you know how I said at the time Mr. Longford would never stand for it?"

Mrs. Barlow nodded.

"And no reason why he should, poor gentleman, with him liking quiet as he does."

Tims shook his head.

"But I was wrong. Miss Shirley's got round him. Coffee is to be served to all three of them in Mr. Longford's room tonight, as Miss Shirley has talked him into listening to a concert."

Daisy could not contain herself; she gave a pleased gasp.

"Well, I am glad; it'll do him a rare lot of good, and . . ."

The look in the eye Mrs. Barlow turned on her would have scared a braver person than Daisy. After a pause Mrs. Barlow said:

"Your opinion was not asked, Daisy, nor wanted."

To the surprise of them all, including herself, Mason broke in.

"I think Daisy's right, though. It's not good for him sitting alone so much. The young ladies have made a great difference in the house, and I think it's more cheerful for us all."

Mrs. Barlow shuddered.

"You only say that, Ada Mason, because Miss Shirley's got round you by giving you that hat. But if you knew the guy you looked in it you wouldn't be so pleased."

Mason was abashed, but courageous.

"I dare say the hat isn't quite right for me, but it's so pretty. I always did want a hat with one of those veils."

Mrs. Barlow made a click with her tongue against her teeth. She looked at Tims.

"There's too many changes going on in this house, and I don't put them down to Miss Shirley. It's that Miss Mayne who is at the bottom of them, I'll be bound. Her sort who gets wages like us down here, but eats in the dining-room, is never up to any good."

This time it was Tims who answered; he wasn't only surprised to find himself doing so, but surprised at the power in his voice. He had spoken quietly for so many years that he did not know he could produce that much volume.

"You've no right to speak that way, Mrs. Barlow. Miss Mayne has never been down here yet and you've never spoken to her, but I see a good deal of her, and one nicer, nor more considerate, you couldn't wish to find."

Mrs. Barlow's tone was acid.

"What about the flower vases? We've heard enough grumbling about them."

Tims stuck to his guns.

"Well, I may have done, and I don't say a lot of flowers dropping on my carpets don't make trouble for somebody, but after all the work falls on the charlady, and if she's nothing to say about it, no more have I."

Mrs. Barlow had never before been outnumbered in an argument at her own kitchen table, and she did not intend to start now. She got up with dignity and looked scornfully down her nose at the lot of them.

"When I came to this house it was a proper place for an establishment servant, but these last weeks I might have been in some second-rate boarding-house. What with you, Ada Mason, singing round the house some rubbish about 'not being too old to dream,' which is a lie if ever I heard one, and you, Mr. Tims, telling Miss Shirley it's a pleasure to clean all her silver, which we who know what you've always had to say about the salver know to be a downright falsehood. And as for you, Daisy, who never have had any sense with your everlasting 'Miss Mayne this' and 'Miss Mayne that', it's enough to make a decent woman sick. But I give you all fair warning, there's some who knows their place and if things go on the way they are I'll take it upon myself to write to Mrs. Cross and then you'll see what's what."

Marda sat across the room and watched Shirley doing her stuff with James. Shirley was a shameless adapter of herself to the needs of the moment. To Marda, who was always herself, Shirley was a revelation. Now, with the need to make James agree to hear the wireless, she was obliterating her tough little self, and producing a childlike creature who would easily dissolve into tears if disappointed.

"Now don't be a nasty old Uncle Jimmie, making up your mind not to like it. I've chosen this specially for you. It's going to be all Negro spirituals. I'll be dreadfully disappointed if you don't think it's swell."

James was obviously restive; he was trying hard, but the unaccustomed company worried him.

"My dear child, why do you think I'll enjoy it?"

Shirley's voice was like a cooing dove's, but her hands were busy fixing the wireless.

"I just know you will. Now listen."

It was a negro choir who were visiting London. They started with an old favourite, "I got shoes . . ." Marda could see that James, untrained to that particular art, was confused by the triumphant voices. She came over to him.

"It's their idea of Heaven," she explained. "You see, they were slaves and only their masters had shoes, so it meant a lot to think all God's children had them."

Shirley was by the wireless. She looked at James and Marda over her shoulder. She saw the nervous pleat between James' eyebrows smooth out as if touched with an iron as Marda spoke, but still more clearly she saw Marda, and with the clearsightedness of an American-educated girl knew things Marda felt, and that Marda never suspected.

The voices of the singers died away. Shirley took advantage of Marda's quieting influence and perched herself on James' chair and laid her arm lightly on his shoulder. The negroes broke robustly into "Joshua fought the battle of Jericho."

James liked that hymn. It had the quality of he-mannishness that had been the keynote of the days when he had his sight; he smiled up at Shirley.

"They certainly can sing, these fellows."

It was a great concession. Shirley gave Marda a smile.

Marda felt a pain in her heart of which she was ashamed. Whatever was coming over her? What a miserable kind of woman she was. She ought to be pleased they were getting James to listen to the concert at all, let alone pleased that he admitted to enjoying it, and here she was feeling in a mood to cry, and all because Shirley had the right to sit on James' chair and put her arm round his neck. Well, why shouldn't she? Wasn't he her guardian? In any case what difference did it make? However much she might like it, her arm would never be round his neck; she was just an employee in the house, nothing more.

After the hymn the choir sang a medley of popular negro songs. "Way down upon the Swanee River" and "Carry me back to old Virginia." Shirley joined in. She had a quite lovely mezzo voice which she used unaffectedly, breaking off in the middle of a line to urge the other two to sing with her. James showed sudden animation.

"No, go on. I like real singing, it's better than all this relayed stuff."

Shirley was delighted to find him amused. She followed the choir into "Poor old Joe." She had an amusing way of helping out the accompaniment with twangings in imitation of a banjo.

Marda listened and watched and struggled with herself. Surely Shirley was a little unfairly loaded with gifts. She was lovely. She had money. She could sing. She could paint. And, according to Clarice, she could play tennis as though she were in training for Wimbledon. She, Marda, seemed very poorly equipped beside her. She was not pretty, she had no money, she could hardly sing a note, she couldn't paint, and she was only moderately good at games. Somehow she had battled her way through her exams to become a dispenser, but that seemed rather a dreary asset against all the gifts Shirley had by nature. She did not indulge in self-pity, for that was foreign to her, but she did draw a mental picture of an exceptionally drab woman.

"I'll just have to be useful," she thought sadly, "for I haven't anything about me to make me anything else."

She was snatched back from her thoughts by James.

"Miss Mayne, Miss Mayne, where are you?"

She loved that particular little-frightened-boy note in his voice; she hurried to him.

"I'm here. What is it?"

He relaxed.

"Nothing, but it's getting late. I thought perhaps you'd slipped off to bed."

Shirley rose from the arm of James' chair and turned off the wireless.

"No, she's here, but I reckon that's enough concert for one night."

James felt he had been ungrateful.

"I wish I had a piano, then you could sing sometimes."

Shirley was on to that like a knife.

"Now that's a dandy idea. I can play my own accompaniments, too. I'll be out in the morning. We could easily get a baby grand in here; there's an awful lot of junk that'll stand throwing out."

James frowned nervously.

"Oh, well—I—"

Marda laid her hand on his arm.

"Don't worry, we won't move you about until you give the word."

Shirley danced forward and gave him a hug.

"That's right, there's no reason why it should come in here until you're ready. Goodnight, Uncle Jimmie, darling, and you did like the singers, didn't you?"

He kissed her.

"Yes—yes, thank you. I enjoyed it—it's just I'm not used—"

Shirley laughed.

"Don't say another word. We understand, but you'll get used, you'll see."

Marda laid her hand in James'.

"Goodnight."

"Goodnight."

Marda walked to the door in a trance. Was she imagining things, or had he held her hand a second; not shaken it, but held it as if he wanted to?

Outside Shirley slipped her arm through Marda's.

"Makes life a whole lot more amusing, I will say."

"What does?"

Shirley looked at her out of the corners of her eyes.

"Two girls fighting it out. I'd say there was a lot of fun in that."

CHAPTER SIX

THE summer holidays were nearly over; the tennis had been a success. In spite of herself, Clarice had to admire Shirley for the way she played, and, with the usual schoolgirl outlook, to admit that a girl who was good at games must be fairly all right as a person. Edward, still dithering in an emotional chaos, lived his days as it were from tennis court to tennis court. He had originally intended only to produce the dullest of the boys he knew, to avoid competition; but his choice had been limited. Most of his friends were away for the holidays and he had to take what he could get; but as the boys returned to London, the news of Shirley got around and the telephone rang at all hours; senior boys he had scarcely spoken to rang up to say in an offhand way that "If there was any tennis going they were about." Pride won over jealousy; Edward could not resist the glory of showing Shirley off.

Marda was delighted to see the tennis idea working out so well. None of the boys at Edward's school were rich, but they could manage a little hospitality, and day after day Shirley was invited to a simple dance with the carpet rolled up, and a gramophone, or supper and a cinema; and once or twice, picnics on Sunday.

Marda also was delighted to see the effect of these amusements on Shirley. Every day it seemed to her the girl was growing much more her age. She looked as lovely as ever, but far less sophisticated. Parties where there were no spirits, and people got tight on laughter, did not fit in with too much make-up or backless frocks.

Marda herself found her evenings long. She would pack Shirley off in a taxi, and then settle down with a book until she came home. But she found it difficult to concentrate on what she was reading. Her mind kept jumping off the page and flying to James sitting alone overhead. Some nights it was all she could do to remain in her chair. It seemed so foolish that two lonely people should not sit together, but she had reasoned the matter out and determined to stand by her reasoning. James knew she was in, Shirley had formed the habit of kissing him goodnight before she went out; if he wanted her company he had only to ring, and if he was too shy and too habit-formed to do that, he could easily say to her when she read to him in the mornings, "If you are alone tonight, come up and read to me, or have a talk." But he never did. It seemed to her that he was like something in a shell: he had been eased half out, but the other half remained obstinately wedged. She was becoming increasingly sensitive to discussing him; but one day, after her dispensing, Alistair brought the subject up, and instead, as was her recent habit, of answering in a dismissing word or two, she laid her worries bare.

"How's your Mr. Longford coming along? We haven't heard much of him lately; is he cheering up at all, poor fellow?"

Perhaps it was the "poor fellow" that loosened Marda's tongue. Her mother and the twins had said things which had made her feel they thought James rather gutless. She quite saw that to outsiders he might seem that, but she could understand so well how he had become as he had, and it hurt her to have him misunderstood.

"He is and he isn't. Shirley has made a marvellous difference. She is used to people liking to see her, and she pops in and out of his room whenever she feels like it."

He leant back in his chair.

"And what about you? I should have thought a dose of you taken three times daily would be a stimulant."

She sat on the edge of his desk.

"I read to him after breakfast, and I've managed a few little things. I see his windows are open—he used to live in a shocking fug—and whether he likes it or not I keep flowers in his room."

"Can't you get him out? Doesn't he ever have any exercise?"

"Not walking. I believe he does a daily dozen—at least so Tims tells me—and he always has a cold bath, I hear. You see, he was a very energetic sort of person and he hasn't slackened in his habits. It's only a horror of being a burden that makes him shut himself up."

He nodded.

"Poor devil!"

Marda warmed to his sympathy.

"When Shirley's home, she makes him have a social evening. She brings in her wireless and we all have coffee together."

"Does he seem to enjoy that?"

She shrugged her shoulders.

"Sometimes, but I think one half of him is protesting all the time. It's as if he was afraid to enjoy anything; and then of course he's been so much alone these last six years that people tire him. Often I see a tightening of his skin—it's as if you could almost feel his nerves tugging. I think then he finds it quite hard to sit still; he'd like to scream."

He looked at her with interest.

"A very good and shrewd description. I daresay he doesn't appreciate it, but he's lucky to have such an understanding person as yourself about."

Marda laughed.

"He appreciates me sometimes. Shirley sings very well, and the first time he heard her he was sufficiently carried away to say so; since then she's ordered a piano, and she's at him day and night to have it put into his room."

Alistair was amused.

"I must say, blind or not, I'd strike at that. I can imagine that young woman on a piano."

Marda fidgeted with her father's tray of pencils.

"It's difficult to know how slow or how fast to move. It's made a pretty considerable change in his life, Shirley and myself coming, anyway, and we've managed to make him see much more of us than he ever meant. But now we seem to have come to a deadlock; we aren't progressing a bit."

Alistair did not answer for a time; when he did it was in the tone in which he discussed a case with a colleague.

"I shouldn't force things. With a patient like that, one suggestion coming from himself is worth fifty from you or Shirley."

It was these words of her father's, together with her own wisdom, which kept Marda sitting alone night after night It was also something else which was hardly a thought, but more subconscious knowledge.

It was not only, or even mostly, for James' sake that she wanted to be with him. She fought her feeling for him partly because such feelings were new to her and scared her, and a little because she knew them useless. She was nothing to James and never would be. She might imagine things, a tone of his voice, a pressure of his hand, but that was the wish forming the thought. But sometimes in the evenings, when Shirley was out, she let her mind free. In imagination she ran up the few stairs that divided them and opened his door, and without waiting to say a word sat where Shirley so often sat, on the arm of his chair, and laid her face against his. His voice as heard in her imagination set her pulses throbbing.

"Is that you, darling?"

Sitting together, she on the arm and he in the chair, she pretended telling him all the things that in reality she must keep shut in her heart. Even in a daydream they spent glorious half-hours together.

Shirley once came home in the middle of one of Marda's dreams; she had opened the door quietly and stood for a second unnoticed, then with a bound she was across the room and kneeling at Marda's feet.

"What were you thinking, honey?"

Marda came back to reality with a start.

"Oh, nothing."

Shirley rubbed her cheek against Marda's knee.

"Lying's a sin and you'll surely go to Hell. Who were you thinking of? I bet he's nice!"

Marda rumpled Shirley's hair.

"Silly goose! Did you have a good evening?"

Shirley nodded.

"But you can't put me off that way." She ran a finger up and down Marda's skirt. "You know you shouldn't sit here all alone. You're only twenty-six, and ought to be having a dandy time."

Marda got up.

"I don't want a dandy time. I'm happy here."

Shirley looked wise.

"That's just it, you shouldn't be. You ought to be mad as a hornet you aren't having your share of fun."

Marda held out a hand to pull Shirley off the floor.

"Well, I'm not. Come on, bedtime."

One night, when Shirley had gone out to dance, a letter came by the evening post for Marda. It was from the art school she had chosen. It seemed she had neglected to fill in some form—would she let the school have it by return of post? She read it through and found that it must be signed by the pupil's guardian. She hesitated quite a time before she took it upstairs. Was it really important James should sign it tonight? Or would it do tomorrow morning? The "return of post" decided her. She knocked at James' door.

James was reading, his fingers moving along the lines of Braille.

"Sorry to interrupt," Marda apologised. "But there's a form just come from Shirley's art school that needs your signature."

He laid aside his book and took a fountain pen out of his pocket.

"This is one of the things I can do. I believe my signature is the same as ever it was."

Marda seldom heard him refer to his blindness.

"Is it difficult to keep straight?"

"No; but I have to be guided to the line to start with. Where do I put it?"

She spread the form out on the table and put his hand on the right place.

"Here."

He signed.

"There, that's straight, isn't it?"

"Yes." She took away the form and folded it. "I'll post this; they want it back right away."

He looked up.

"Ring for Tims; he'll take it."

Marda addressed the envelope while a hope quivered in her. He had not just said "Give it to Tims," he had said "Ring for Tims." He looked almost as if he were not expecting her to go right away.

Marda waited until Tims had taken the letter before she said casually:

"Well, goodnight."

James made a slight movement.

"Oh, goodnight—I mean, isn't it early?"

Marda, in spite of a heart beating so loudly she thought James must hear it, managed to sound very matter-of-fact.

"Yes, quite. I'll stay a minute or two, shall I? I'm alone downstairs; Shirley's out." He was obviously shy now he had made his request, so she hurried on. "I've had an idea about Shirley's piano. If we put it in her sitting-room you could hear it quite well up here if ever you wanted to, or perhaps some evening you could come down."

He considered her words in evident surprise.

"Yes. Well—yes, I could. I suppose there's no reason why I shouldn't."

"Of course there isn't," she went on cheerfully, "and it would please her."

He paused again; then he spoke quickly.

"I've been thinking about a wireless. There's no reason why I couldn't work one myself. I'd soon learn. I should only use it for the news."

Marda carefully kept her pleasure out of her voice.

"Of course you could. There are a lot of good talks, too. I daresay you wouldn't often want to hear one, but you might now and again."

He relaxed a little.

"Would you go and choose one for me?"

"Yes. I'll do it tomorrow."

"Thank you." He gave a rather sheepish smile. "I've always set my face against having one, but since Shirley has been bringing hers in I've thought I wouldn't mind having one by me."

Marda looked at his book.

"What are you reading?"

He turned scarlet.

"Matter of fact, it's part of the Bible. Some of it's awfully good reading."

Marda disguised her surprise. The Bible was the last book she would have pictured him with.

"Which part?"

"The Song of Solomon." He frowned. "I've never been much of a hand at this Braille reading, I'm so damned slow."

"It's one of the loveliest books," said Marda. "I love the part that begins 'I am the rose of Sharon.'"

His sightless eyes gazed across the room at her.

"That was what I was reading."

She had a good memory and quoted:

"'I am the rose of Sharon, and the lily of the valleys. As the lily among thorns, so is my love among the daughters. As the apple tree among the trees of the wood, so is my beloved among the sons. I sat down under his shadow with great delight, and his fruit was sweet to my taste. He brought me to the banqueting house, and his banner over me was love. Stay me with flagons, comfort me with apples: for I am sick of love.'"

James made a movement and an ivory bookmarker fell on the floor. Marda jumped up and returned it, thankful for the interruption, for the words she was quoting had made her tremble. As she straightened herself, James held out his hand; almost unconsciously she took it.

"Marda," he whispered, and laid his other hand over hers, "your voice is so lovely."

"I'm glad." She moved towards him so that there should not be even a suggestion she was pulling away. "You see, I so want to help you."

"You do. More than you can believe possible. That's what I was reading the Bible for. I knew there was a verse somewhere that described how I feel now you are in the house."

"Which is it?"

"'For, lo, the winter is past, the rain is over and gone; the flowers appear on the earth; the time of the singing of birds is come.'"

She knelt down beside him.

"But the winter could be much more past, and more flowers could appear, and more birds could sing, if only you wouldn't shut yourself away, but come out and hear the voice of the turtle in our land."

His fingers began to stroke hers.

"I'd only be a burden."

"Rubbish! That's a creed you've frightened yourself into believing. When you were a child, wasn't there a cupboard or a cistern that scared you, and it was only after years you knew you'd imagined its terrors? That's how it is with you. There's no disability on this earth that courage can't ride over."

He gripped her hand.

"I suppose I do look a coward to you, but you didn't know me before. I was spoilt, I dare say. I was lucky at all sports, and women were nice to me, and I had a grand time. Then I had my accident. I couldn't let my friends come round pawing and sympathising."

She twisted her hand so that she was holding his.

"Wasn't that a bit mean to the friends?"

"No. There was no room in their lives for a crock. They'd have made room, but I knew how they'd have felt."

"But is that any reason to shut yourself up in one room? You could walk about your own house. And we could get a car and go out into the country; it smells lovely at this time of year with the bracken just turning."

He shied like a scared horse.

"People will stare."

"Why should they? Your face isn't scarred. Besides, there are a great many blind people about. My father uses blind masseuses for his patients, and they come and go like anybody else."

He nodded.

"I know, but I can't bring myself to do that. I can hear them all, 'Look, there's poor old Jimmie; one of us ought to go and give him a cheerio.'"

Marda's voice was pleading.

"I think you ought to bring yourself to it. You needn't go to your clubs and things if you don't want to, but there are other places. Will you try?"

His face twitched.

"I can't be rushed."

"Nobody is going to rush you."

"I won't see my friends."

"Well, you needn't. You needn't see anybody but myself and Shirley."

He was plainly struggling.

"Well, perhaps some time. I might go and have a sniff at the country."

It was a big concession. Unconsciously she had been holding her breath, now she let it go.

"That's grand." With a squeeze at his hand she got up. "Well, I must go down and be ready for Shirley. Goodnight."

He held her.

"Goodnight, Marda."

He sat listening, straining to hear her footsteps cross the room, then as the door shut he relaxed.

Marda went down to the sitting-room. It was a warm night and she opened the window and looked out into the Square. She felt as if hours had passed since she had left the room. Emotionally, the situation was so changed. Looking up at the stars, she took deep breaths and tried to think clearly. What did it mean exactly? He had said that she helped him more than she could believe possible; he had. said that now she was in the house it was as if the winter was past and the time of the singing of birds had come. But did that mean anything more than that a desperately lonely blind man had found pleasure in a little companionship? All of Marda's senses longed to answer, 'Yes; it means that it's you personally that have made the difference. He cares for you; perhaps in time he'll love you.' But her common sense would not listen to such talk.

"Don't be such an idiot. You're being like a sloppy school-girl. Just now, because he's coming to life a bit, he thinks he has you to thank; but when he gets around and meets people, you'll just go back to where you belong, in fact you'll be what you are, a paid companion."

Marda was still stargazing when Shirley came home.

"Taking up astrology?" Shirley asked.

Marda laughed.

"No. It's just a lovely night and I was looking at it. Your art school has sent in a form which Mr. Longford had to sign. I think by tomorrow you'll be on the register."

"That's fine!" Shirley took off her coat. "Did Uncle Jimmie sign it? I've never seen him write. I thought maybe he couldn't, being blind."

"Yes. I showed him where to, of course. You've broken him in; he says he'll have a wireless."

"My!" Shirley was quite startled. "He is coming on. Did he say anything else, any other signs of breaking out?"

For a second Marda hesitated.

"No. No other signs. What about us going to bed?"

Marda woke up to the consciousness of a gaiety of heart. For a few seconds she did not know what had caused this; then, like a gentle wave sliding over the sand, the memory of yesterday swept over her. She lay for a while letting it engulf her, remembering every word said last night, the tone of James' voice, the feel of his fingers; then her practical common sense came to the front. What an idiot she was! This sort of daydreaming was just what she had scolded herself for last night, and decided not to give in to.

"I tell you what, my girl," she told herself severely, "you need stiffening. You'll have a cold bath, and after breakfast you'll have that long-delayed talk with Mrs. Barlow."

Marda loathed cold baths and never took them except as a self-imposed corrective. She wasted no time on this one, but came out gasping after a few minutes. But, as is the way of cold baths, the effect of it was to make her glow, and the more she glowed the less could she check her radiant happiness.

Shirley was not fond of getting up in the morning, but now that her art school was looming in front of her, Marda had persuaded her that she had better start the habit of coming down to breakfast. Today she came down, yawning, in hurriedly-pulled-on slacks and shirt.

"Oh my, I'm tired!"

Marda poured her out a cup of coffee.

"Drink that and you'll feel better. I want to have a talk with you about food. I'm going to see Mrs. Barlow presently."

Shirley opened her eyes.

"My! From what Mason says, she's the big, bad wolf all right."

"I know. But I must. I've been putting off seeing her ever since I've been in the house, and the food is really too depressing. I must see you have things you like."

Shirley helped herself to a piece of toast.

"I'll say it's depressing. I'd like some orange juice for breakfast as a start. And this toast is just terrible."

Marda was eating sausages.

"You ought to take to hearty English breakfasts like me."

Shirley looked at her languidly, then her attention was focused. She laid down her knife and rested her chin on her hands.

"Say, what have you been doing? Having a beauty treatment?"

Marda could not stop herself flushing.

"No, you idiot. Why?"

"Something has done you a bit of good. You look swell."

"Rubbish!"

Shirley went on staring.

"Your eyes have a shine in them, your skin looks different, your hair has more colour." She went thoughtfully back to her toast, and after eating a moment said casually: "Did you sit around with Uncle Jimmie last night after he'd signed that entrance form you told me about?"

Marda's heart gave a leap that would not have disgraced a kangaroo.

"Just a bit—not long."

Shirley reached out for the marmalade.

"It's surprising how time slips away without one noticing."

Marda looked at Shirley's bland expression; did she mean anything by that remark? Undecided, she changed the subject:

"Now about this food business."

It was Daisy who first saw Marda coming to the kitchen. Knowing all Mrs. Barlow had said, she was so scared she could not even say good morning, but gave a little squeak and pushed a piece of her apron against her mouth and ran into the scullery. Marda, with her chin very high to hide a beating heart, knocked on the kitchen door.

Mrs. Barlow opened the door. She had so long been expecting Marda and planning what she would do when she came, that now she saw her she was mentally winded.

"Yes?"

Marda smiled.

"Good morning. I thought it was time we met. Mr. Longford told me to have a talk with you about Miss Shirley's food."

Mrs. Barlow had regained her confidence and with it her truculence.

"You can leave that to me. I was cook to Mr. Longford's uncle and aunt, before he came here, and I think by now I know what's what."

Marda disliked standing in the passage, but Mrs. Barlow was barring the kitchen door, so she had no choice.

"Miss Shirley's rather a special proposition," she explained, refusing to show she noticed Mrs. Barlow's annoyance. "You see, she's been in America lately and got used to American food."

Mrs. Barlow looked grim.

"Then it's high time she got back to English."

Marda took a firmer note.

"Well, there are a few special things I want put on her menu. I had better give you a list of them."

Mrs. Barlow held out her hand.

"I don't mind having the list, but I'm in charge of this kitchen and what's eaten upstairs has always been left to me."

"I know." Marda's voice had an edge to it. "And because you've been here so long I don't want to do what Mr. Longford suggested, which is to see you daily and order the meals."

Mrs. Barlow's face turned purplish.

"For that I would never stand."

Marda smiled.

"Don't be foolish. You know it's no good talking like that. You and I have got to work together, and I'm sure we'll get on all right."

Mrs. Barlow took a deep breath through her nose. She gave the effect of a toy balloon blown up too full and likely to explode.

"Over my dead body will I have interference in my kitchen. Mr. Longford may be weak, but there are others that will see differently."

Marda had lost all fear. She just regretted that she had to deal with so great a fool, but she had met Mrs. Barlow's like before in her father's surgery. She refused to go on with the discussion.

"Well, there's the list. Fruit juice for Miss Shirley for break-fast and a list of her favourite dishes. I shall expect one of those dishes to appear every other day for the present; if they don't, I shall have to see Mr. Longford about it. I know he would hate to dismiss so old a servant, but Miss Shirley is his ward and her tastes must be considered. Good morning."

In the hall, Marda metaphorically wiped her forehead.

"Phew! What a woman!" She looked round for the papers. She could not see James' favourite, but she picked up a bundle of the rest and turned to climb the stairs. On the bottom step she paused to clarify her mind. How was she going to meet him this morning? Would she go on as a matter of course from where they had left off last night? It was a delicious thought; it would be Heaven to come in and take his hand and make him laugh about Mrs. Barlow. Reflection showed that the answer did not rest with her. Last night was probably an emotional moment; he might be regretting it. She would come in just as usual and leave their reactions to each other for him to decide.

James' door was shut, and as usual Marda knocked and walked straight in. In the doorway she stopped, hurt as she did not know she was capable of being hurt. On a stool at James' feet sat Shirley, a paper on her knee. She was reading it. She stopped in the middle of a sentence and looked up with all the outrageous innocence of which her Madonna face was capable.

"Oh, hullo! I'm reading to Uncle Jimmie this morning. I guess jobs like this are just made for a ward."

CHAPTER SEVEN

MARDA had never known what it was to feel jealous. She had often been pleasantly envious, but without a tinge of any sensa-tion that hurt. In the days that followed Shirley's taking over the morning readings she suffered unendingly. She suffered more because she recognised from the beginning that jealousy was a disease rather than a sin, that it was like a growth which, if not cut out from the start, went on expanding until it forced all decent qualities out of the body. To recognise an enemy, and all that enemy is capable of doing to you, is an advantage in the battle to come, but there is still the battle to be won. Marda fought hers grimly, sometimes losing, but more often gaining. She was not helped by the fact that there was no sign from James that he cared. He never mentioned the change of readers, though Shirley read badly and with American inflexions. He appeared not to mind that now he had little or no privacy; Shirley popped in and out of his room at all hours. Shirley became increasingly easy in her manner with him, perching herself on his chair as a matter of course, often patting or caressing him, and he showed none of his old restlessness; it was almost as if he liked it. Also she dropped the "Uncle"; he was always just "Jimmie" to her now.

Marda, lying awake at nights, turned and churned these things over in her head. Surely that one lovely evening could not have been induced only by loneliness, surely he must have meant a little by it. Or was he coming to life because of Shirley in the house, and had she been given those minutes of warmth and affection because Shirley, to whom they belonged, was out? In any case, she was being a poor sort of person to mind. She had said to Doctor Ewart that she was going to get James back on his feet; well, wasn't he getting on his feet? Ought she to care how it happened, so long as it happened? She knew that Shirley was not interested in James except that he was a man, and she expected every man to fall for her. Probably he was falling, and that might not be a bad cure, unrequited love hurt, it might be the counter-irritant that his lethargy needed. Shirley was a minx, of course, but a very nice little minx. All this playing around with affections was a game to her; she could not know that she, Marda, was idiot enough to have let herself care desperately, so desperately that every time Shirley went in to see James it hurt like a stitch dragging at a wound, and that more nights than not she cried herself to sleep.

Marda woke up one morning to find her battle won. She had stayed awake until the early hours fighting it out, and found that if she faced the facts fairly she was hurt as if she were bruised inside, but she was no longer jealous.

"I love him," she admitted, sitting up in bed and hugging her knees. "I can't help it. I love him now and I always will, but there's no reason why he should love me. Of course, he can't see me, so he doesn't know I'm plain; in fact, thanks to Shirley's description, he thinks I'm a raving beauty. But he would know all right if he was caring for me at all; that has nothing to do with eyes. But you mustn't blame Shirley, for what she says and does could not affect his feeling for you, if he had any. Shirley's only a child, and playing about with men's feelings is natural to her. She doesn't care twopence about him really, and it would be a mistake if she did—a blind man old enough to be her father is not the man for her; but because of her he may remember what a lot of fun there is in the world outside and go back to it. Take a grip on yourself, Marda, and be grateful for Shirley; she may be able to do for him what you alone could never have managed. Besides that, you are lucky to be in love. Lots of people go through life and never know how it feels to know nothing matters except one person. It's worth while to know, even if it hurts." Two tears dripped off her nose; she brushed them away angrily. "So let's hear no more of this idiocy. Be glad about Shirley, and pull yourself together."

A battle won, if you have the strength to stand at all, leaves an uplifted feeling. Marda, with blue stains under her eyes and a very white face, came down to breakfast, conscious of a serenity of heart. Shirley in a housecoat seemed to have got out of bed the wrong side and scowled at her orange juice.

"That Mrs. Barlow just runs round London looking for oranges so sour I can't drink them."

Marda poured out Shirley's coffee.

"I'll see her about it."

Shirley scowled more ferociously.

"Don't you ever go in for a little wholesome grumbling? You know, I don't want you facing the old she-devil about a thing like that. I guess the oranges aren't as bad as I said."

Marda smiled.

"Good! I don't want to go down and complain before I must. I'm afraid when I do I'll have to ask Mr. Longford to dismiss her."

Shirley took a piece of toast.

"Why didn't you come and have your coffee with Jimmie last night?"

Marda's voice was casual.

"No reason particularly; but he had you there and I had some letters to write. Did he enjoy your playing to him?" Shirley staked a pat of butter.

"It's kind of dumb playing downstairs with him upstairs. I didn't play long."

Marda sipped her coffee.

"I do sympathise with him not wanting the piano in his room. After all, you might want to play things he wouldn't care for."

Shirley spread her toast.

"I'll say I might. He doesn't care for anything swung. He said, would I learn things for him? That was a bit of a knock-out. I hate practising." She raised her eyes. "He asked where you were."

Marda kept her voice level. She would not question Shirley as to what exactly James had said.

"You won't have much time for practising after Monday, when your art school opens."

Shirley put down her cup.

"I guess I'm not going to that place."

Marda was surprised.

"Not! But why?"

Shirley lay back in her chair.

"I kind of think I'd rather hang around here."

Marda's heart missed a beat. What was this? This was not the usual Shirley. Surely the child was not really interested in James. She had no time to work out the difficulties of that possibility. Argument was never effective with Shirley, so she answered casually:

"All right. It's up to you to do what you like."

Shirley's eyes raked Marda's face.

"Have you had a talk about it with Jimmie?"

Marda did not know what she meant.

"No. I thought you were starting on Monday. This is the first time I've heard that you weren't."

Shirley pleated her table napkin.

"I don't see why he should care if I go or not."

Marda agreed.

"I don't suppose he does."

Shirley flung down the napkin and got up.

"Well, he does. I told him last night I'd changed my mind about going, and he acted as if I was breaking the law. He said I'd got to go."

Marda was amazed.

"Really! How odd!"

Shirley was by the window, idly swinging the blind cord to and fro.

"Maybe it's not so odd. Maybe you and he want to be on your own."

Marda's breath was knocked out of her; then, as the full realisation of what Shirley was getting at swept over her, she began to laugh. She laughed until the tears were pouring down her cheeks.

"Oh dear, this is silly."

Shirley's face was glued to the window.

"Glad you find it so funny."

Marda was sobered by her voice. She got up and went to the window and put a hand on Shirley's shoulder.

"Don't be a goose."

Shirley had stiffened at the feel of Marda's arm; then she let go and her polish and self-control vanished, and she flung herself on Marda, sobbing.

"I guess I must have gone crackers, but I can't help myself. I'm crazy about that man."

Marda stroked her hair.

"But, darling, he's the same age as your father was."

"Don't I know?" Shirley choked. "But, you see, it isn't anything new. I was crazy on him when I was a kid. Maybe I was a bit advanced for ten, but I was honest to God in love."

Shirley's face was well buried, so Marda's smile did not matter, her voice was gentle.

"But, darling, there's nothing to cry about."

Shirley spoke in a sob.

"I'm not so sure. I expect I'm every kind of a darned fool, but he just gets me. He's so good-looking and so kind of pathetic, I just want to take him in my arms and look after him for ever."

Marda's face was grave.

"I didn't know you felt like this."

Shirley sniffed.

"Nor did I. It all seemed like a bit of fun at first, the way meeting men always does. Then when I saw you getting all starry-eyed, I thought, well, maybe he's more fun than he seems, and I broke in on your racket, read the paper, and fixed his flowers, and turned on his radio, and then found I was always hanging around and not wanting to go any other place. And then yesterday, when I'd been singing to him and I came up and asked him if he'd like that, he said, 'Where's Miss Mayne?' Well, that kind of got me, and I said I'd fixed I wouldn't go to any fool art school, but he said I must, so then I knew he didn't care a darn. He just wants you round the place."

Marda heard Tims coming along the passage. She caught hold of Shirley's chin and raised her face.

"Pull yourself together. Here's Tims coming. Come in the other room and we'll have a talk about this."

In Shirley's sitting-room, Marda sat on the sofa and drew Shirley down beside her, and waited while, with much mopping and nose-blowing, the girl pulled herself together. Presently Shirley looked up with a wan smile. "Better. Sorry. I guess I'm just plumb jealous."

Marda gazed round the sitting-room, her mind searching for something to say. The room, decorated to Shirley's taste, was now all white and blue; it had a cloistered air, with an over-lay of the big world. Marda had mentally decided it was like a niche for a saint with a cocktail in it instead of a saint. Now it helped her; it made her see Shirley not as a sobbing seven-teen-year-old, in love for the first time, but as the tough little worldling she really was. She tucked an arm through the girl's.

"I think you must have got your liver out of order. What is all this jealousy talk? You and I aren't fighting for your guard-ian, you know."

Shirley looked at her.

"Aren't we?"

Marda, safe with her own battle won and behind her, was able to return the look.

"No."

"But you're fond of him. Maybe in love with him."

Marda was not going to lie.

"Yes, I'm fond of him, but I mean nothing in his life. You know that."

Shirley's eyes were glued to Marda's.

"But you hope to be. That's what you're pushing me off to the art school for."

Marda was angry.

"That's not fair. This art school was arranged for nothing but your own happiness, and you know it."

Shirley had the grace to be ashamed.

"Don't get mad with me. But you see, I never knew a man I couldn't get round if I wanted to. Seems like something is holding Jimmie back, and I think it must be you."

Marda's heart could not help lifting, but her voice was matter-of-fact.

"I'm sure it's nothing to do with me. He's very fond of you."

Shirley nodded knowingly.

"That's just it, fond like he'd be of a child, but I want him crazy."

Marda managed some sort of laugh.

"What d'you want me to do about it?"

Shirley hesitated.

"I want you to leave him to me. I mean if we can really get him to go for a drive or anything, I don't want you taking him while I'm at art school."

Marda locked her hands on her knees.

"All right. I won't suggest it. I promise you."

"You see what I mean, you'll keep out of his way." She laid a hand on Marda's. "I dare say I sound kind of selfish, but you see from the way he's acting I guess he could get fond of me just the way I want."

Marda longed to say "What do you mean?" but she held it back, and instead got up.

"You're a funny child. Now go and powder that red nose and then take the papers up and read them to your Jimmie."

Shirley went to the door, then she stopped.

"Can you come shopping later? I've got to buy that song Jimmie wants to hear."

Marda agreed, her tone for all her effort sounding dead. "What is it?"

Shirley rummaged in her pocket and brought out a scrap of paper.

"It's called 'Passing By'; it's by Purcell."

Marda stood where she was for quite a while after the door shut, puzzling over her position. What would be the sensible thing to do? Her common sense said, "Leave. Don't risk squabbling with the girl over the man." The mere thought of such a thing vulgarised everything. But she knew she wouldn't leave. There was happiness in being even in the same house with him. One thing she was certain she was not going to do, and that was to make any effort with James. Shirley had a funny little mind, she might or she might not really be in love, but she should have the field to herself. There was something terribly distasteful in the idea of the paid companion being accused of trying to get off with her employer.

Marda pushed her hair off her face and squared her shoulders. She felt the better for having made a clear decision; but for all her oneness of purpose, two things worried her. What did Shirley mean by "The way he's acting I guess he could get fond of me the way I want"? Had she, too, had her hand held, and been told that because of her the time of the singing of birds had come? And why did he want Shirley to sing "Passing By"?

On Monday Shirley went off to her art school. Having had her scene with Marda over James, she seemed to put the subject out of her mind. Marda did not know whether this was due to trust in herself, or to Shirley's volatile spirits which had a sorbo-ball quality—she did not care for dents on her surface, preferring to smooth them out immediately they appeared. But for whatever reason, she went off to her art school in great form, taking immense care over her make-up and clothes.

"I do hope they realise," Marda remarked, "that you've not come to work."

Shirley giggled.

"It'll be a funny school that makes a slave out of me."

With Shirley out of the house, Marda picked up the newspapers. She did not know whether she was dreading the moment or looking forward to it. She had not seen James alone since the night he had held her hand. Always Shirley had been in the room. She had not let herself imagine this meeting; she thought preconceived ideas about what either he or she would do or say were a mistake. She knew a cool friendliness must be her attitude, in face of her promise to Shirley, but how she would maintain it if there was even a gesture from him, she could not imagine. She steadied herself mentally as she climbed the stairs.

"Keep a hold on yourself. It'll probably be perfectly easy."

She opened James' door. He was standing at the window. She was glad to hear his wireless on, a cheerful blare coming from Radio Normandy. He switched it off as she came in.

"Who's that?"

Marda did not know if she was Marda or Miss Mayne to him.

"It's me."

He felt his way towards her.

"Oh, my dear. I am glad. I have missed your reading. Shirley is a darling, but her voice!"

Marda stood where she was, struggling not to go to him, and not to let her gladness sound in her tone.

"She likes doing it for you, though."

He stood still, a listening expression on his face.

His next words came with far less eagerness.

"But you are going to read this morning?"

"Of course. I'll start now, shall I?"

Without a word he turned and felt his way to his chair.

Marda looked at him miserably. She felt she had hurt him, that he had hoped for some warmth. She felt that between her own feelings and Shirley's and not knowing how he felt, or if he felt at all, she was making a muddle. Angry with herself, she sat down and opened the paper.

She read for nearly an hour. At the end, James thanked her.

"That was grand." He fidgeted with his tie. "I've been wanting to see you. I wanted a chance to tell you I've been thinking over what you said the other night. I don't want to go about amongst people I knew, but I might try a day in the country and get around a bit more. I was looking out just now, seems fine. What about this afternoon?"

Marda looked at the cloudless sky and could not bring herself to lie to him.

"That'll be grand. But I must try and get hold of Shirley; she'll hate not to be there on your first drive."

He looked as if he were going to say something in a hurry, but he changed his mind. There was quite a pause before he answered:

"Let's leave it until tomorrow, then. Of course I meant Shirley to come."

Marda got up.

"Shall I turn your wireless on?"

He shook his head.

"I can manage. I don't feel like it just now, anyhow."

Downstairs Marda slammed the newspapers on to their table.

"Oh goodness, I can feel I've made a mess of that. I expect he's been embarrassed about letting himself go the other night and was waiting to put things right, and I was so clumsy I've only managed to build a wall between us. I am a mutt."

Marda hired a Daimler, and they drove to Crockham Hill, where there were miles of more or less deserted woods in which to walk. Shirley sat on one side of James and Marda on the other. Marda had planned to sit by the chauffeur, but James protested.

"Where are you, Marda?"

She flushed at the "Marda."

"I don't want to crush you."

"But you won't, will she, Shirley?"

Marda looked at Shirley anxiously, wondering how she would react to both the Marda and the arrangement. But Shirley, whatever she might feel, seemed composed. "Course not. Come on—tons of room for three."

It was six years since James had driven in a car, except when he had been brought to Thurloe Square after his accident. They had scarcely been going a minute before Marda realised he was suffering tortures from nerves. She could feel his arm touching hers twitch and his whole body contract. It seemed to her so natural that a man who had always driven should be nervous at being driven while he himself could not see, that had she and James been alone she would have brought the subject up, and tried to help him by accepting how he felt. But with Shirley in the car, her tongue was tied. Shirley had travelled an immense amount by air and thought of cars as a slow, dull way of getting about. She was not the type to be imaginative about that sort of thing; no man, in her view, was ever nervous.

As an acutely sensitive person, Marda suffered in another's suffering, apart from the fact that the suffering in this case was James'. She could not enjoy herself while someone else was wretched. She bore his discomfort for a time, and then, as the car swung round a bend and James turned quite pale, she did what she would have done to a frightened child, she slipped her hand under the rug stretched over their knees and held his hand. She was startled at the effect. For a second he gripped it as if it were a bush and he falling over a cliff, then his fingers relaxed, and so did his body. Marda was reminded of rain after a thunderstorm—that was the effect her hand seemed to have. All the tension gone and something more than calm taking its place.

Shirley had kept up a gay rattle of conversation ever since they had started. She was telling them about the art school. It appeared it was full of funny types, each of which she described in a few neat words. She seemed so intent on what she was saying that she had no time to see what was happening to the other two. But that was an illusion. Shirley was never too busy to see things which concerned her. She noticed the swerve at the corner and the slight movement as Marda's hand slid into James'. By not a flutter of an eyelash nor a change in the tempo of her conversation did she show that she had seen, but a quarter of a mile farther on she pulled his other hand outside the rug and on to her knee and there openly held it and played with his fingers.

Marda was horrified; of course Shirley would think she was holding James' hand for affection—what else could she think? After a moment or two, so that James would not connect her movement with Shirley's, she began to withdraw her hand. But there she met with a surprise; James would not let it go; his fingers closed round hers like a trap. She could not struggle; she had to leave her hand quiescent. With an excitement she couldn't keep down, Marda felt those fingers. She did not know what his grip meant—whether he needed the confidence she gave him, or whether he wanted to hold it because it gave him pleasure—but she did know that because he was now holding her hand, and not she, in a capacity of nurse, holding his, all the platonicness of the situation, from her point of view, had gone.

They stopped for lunch at an inn. James would not eat in front of anybody; he had a horror that now that he could not see he might eat untidily. For him there were sandwiches and a flask in the car. The two girls lunched together. In the tiny congested cloakroom where they went to powder their noses, Shirley turned on Marda.

"That's a funny way to show that you don't care for a man, holding his hand under a rug."

Marda made up her lips.

"If you had not been so busy talking, you'd have known he was scared stiff. That was why I held it."

"Oh, yeah?"

"It's true."

"What's he scared of?"

Marda hated stupidity.

"Just imagine how you'd feel dashing through space when you couldn't see, and don't forget he's probably hardly been in a car since his accident."

Shirley thought this over.

"Oh! Well, are you telling me you didn't enjoy it?"

Marda shook her head.

"I'm not telling you anything except why I held his hand, and I wouldn't tell you that only I don't want another of your big scenes in which you accuse me of stealing the affection of the only man you ever loved."

Shirley powdered her nose in angry dabs.

"I just don't seem to know how we're fixed. Why couldn't he let you sit in front with the chauffeur? And why's he taken to calling you Marda?"

"As for sitting in front, that was probably politeness; and as for calling me Marda, why shouldn't he? I can't be Miss Mayne for ever."

"Do you call him Jimmie?"

Marda's eyes twinkled.

"No, and I don't suppose I ever will. When I stop calling him Mr. Longford, he'll be just Jim, or James."

Shirley put her lipstick and powder back in her bag. "Funny thing is I can't get really mad with you. I kind of like you, however you act."

Marda opened the door.

"And I like you. Let's go and have that lunch."

The woods when they reached them were looking lovely. They took James down a wide ride where the horses had beaten the leaf-mould and pine needles flat and there were no tree-stumps for him to fall over. The bracken was beginning to turn golden, and so was the beech. And from the wood came the rich pungency of the beginning of autumn.

James, with Shirley holding one arm and Marda the other, walked in silence. He walked slowly and hesitatingly, but his face was rapt and his nose lifted like a hound finding the scent.

"Lord," he exclaimed suddenly, "this is grand." He turned to Marda. "I can see it all. There's a flash of grey as a squirrel runs up a tree, isn't there? And a white blob of a rabbit's tail, and perhaps a cock pheasant strutting amongst the undergrowth."

She was so pleased at his enthusiasm that she unconsciously hugged his arm to her.

"That's right. The leaves are turning a bit; they're early this year."

Shirley yawned.

"It looks like any old wood to me."

James smiled.

"Hark at you, you town bred miss. I remember when you were a kid taking you up on Beachy Head, and you said, 'Have we come all this way to look at a lot of grass?'"

Shirley rubbed her cheek against his shoulder. "You remember quite a lot about me."

He nodded.

"Quite a lot." He turned back to Marda. "She could twist me round her little finger then, and I expect she can still."

Marda felt as if the sun had suddenly gone in. Quickly she released her arm from James'.

"Look at these blackberries. I must eat some."

James and Shirley walked on slowly.

"You keep your eyes on the road," James said to her anxiously. "I've not done any country walks, and I don't want to fall on my nose."

Shirley held him closer to her.

"You won't. You can't do better than have me by you." Marda watched them with a lump in her throat.

She had picked a few blackberries, but she forgot to eat them; instead, they rolled unheeded from her hand on to the pine needles.

CHAPTER EIGHT

THAT expedition was like the turning of a key in a rusty lock. Slowly, creakingly, but surely, the door of James' life opened. Every day something new found room to get in. Having walked in a wood in the country, it was a natural step to a walk in the Park. Having let Shirley make a habit of popping in and out of his room, it became ridiculous to confine himself to the one sitting-room, as if he were an invalid, so in no time he was all over the house. He could not break himself of feeling agonisingly self-conscious eating in public, but having coffee with the two girls became a matter of course. He still preferred his cluttered ugly room to Shirley's sitting-room; he said her room smelt so clean he was afraid to smoke in it, but he sat there sometimes to hear her play, though more often they sat in his room after dinner. Shirley tried to get him to come to a musical play or a music hall, but at that he struck. One of his nightmares was of being led into a public place and greeted by an old friend and hearing pity in his voice. However, she did manage to get him to play cards. She bought two braille packs and, with a view to bridge later on, taught him Rummy, giving him plenty of time to finger the cards and learn to read their value quickly. James had at first jibbed at the idea, saying he had always hated cards, and anyway was a fool at braille and would never learn to use them. But after a night or two he was enjoying himself, and quite late he and Shirley were still at it, fighting out who owed who half a crown.

Marda deliberately took the smallest share in all this. Only the morning readings and sometimes the walks concerned her. She found even these difficult to manage in accordance with her conscience. Somehow, in spite of herself, and, as far as she could see, in spite of James, and with very little that was personal said, an intimacy was established. She, watching his face and noting a nervous twitch of his fingers or a tightening of his muscles, had a silent understanding of, and with him, far more binding than things said. And he, with steadily growing sensitiveness to her, not only knew when she was in or out of a room, but seemed to know her feelings as if he were a barometer and she the weather.

Marda worried and puzzled over herself and James. Only so rarely did he show any outward sign that he liked having her about; all that he reserved for Shirley. It was for her his face lit up when the door opened, and to her he called out "Hullo, Minx." It was she that he seemed to want near him, petting her and teasing her. Only once did he show any sign of the man who had held Marda's hand and quoted the "Song of Songs." It was the night that Shirley had learnt for him "Passing By." She was downstairs playing it, and her rich husky voice floated up the stairs.

"... *Was never face so pleas'd my mind;*
I did but see her passing by,
And yet I love her till I die."

Like a break in a dam and the water pouring through, James's voice burst from him.

"Marda!—Marda!" and he held out his hand.

It was all Marda could do not to go to him. The longing to touch him, perhaps even to kiss him, hurt like a throb from a wound, but she stayed where she was. She had given Shirley her word, it would be insufferable if the girl came upstairs after having sung to please him, to find, or even to suspect, that he had been holding her hand.

"Her gestures, motions, and her smile,
Her wit, her voice, my heart beguile . . ."

"Yes, what is it?" Marda's voice was a whisper; she could not force it to more.

"Beguile my heart I know not why,
And yet I love her till I die!"

James seemed to shrink in size, all eagerness left him. The hand he had held out dropped in a lonely, frustrated way to his knees.

"Cupid is winged, and doth range
Her country. So my heart doth change . . ."

Marda fought against a lump in her throat which felt like a cricket ball. To hurt the feelings of anyone was bad, but to hurt a blind man's . . . Quickly she got up and crept out on the landing.

"But change the earth or change the sky,
Yet will I love her till I die!"

Shirley came bounding up the stairs; she saw Marda's disappearing back.

"Hullo, off to bed already?"

Tears were by now streaming down Marda's cheeks, and she had no power to stop them. She hurried on, giving a vague nod and muttering:

"Nose is bleeding."

Because she could not say the things to James she longed to say, Marda usually talked to him of domestic things. Through her he got an entirely new view of his household.

"Of course, I think Tims was quite a dog once. I should think your Uncle George and Aunt Lettice were pretty flattening to work for. They've kind of squashed the vitality out of him."

They were walking in Kensington Gardens when she said this. James turned an amused face to her.

"Old Tims with a past! That's good."

"Oh, I don't mean anything so concrete as a past. More likely he cherishes a garter kicked off by a lady in a music-hall singing 'Ta-ra-raboom-de-ay' in the nineties."

James chuckled.

"And a valentine or two, do you think?"

"I shouldn't wonder. Of course I think there's a little life in him yet. You know, the other day I came down early to breakfast and he was reading the paper so intently he didn't hear me. He put it down directly he saw me and said something about 'just wondering how the international situation was this morning.' But after he'd gone I turned the paper over to see what he had been reading, and the heading was 'The best of the dogs tonight.'"

"Greyhound racing! Tims!"

"Well, I wouldn't say he went. But I think perhaps he puts a bit on with somebody."

"Really! You know he's looked after me for six years, and in all that time he's never said anything more original than 'Nip in the air this morning, sir. Winter's drawing on.'"

Marda could imagine Tims and James during the six years only too well.

"But, you see, that was partly because of you. You've no idea how your getting about a bit, and having Shirley in the house, is affecting all the staff, except of course Mrs. Barlow. It's just like the story of 'Sleeping Beauty.' You remember all the palace servants went to sleep at what they were doing, and when the spell was broken they woke up and started living again. That's how it is in your house. You should see Mason in the hat Shirley has given her. She came to me to know if it was too flighty. She looked a scream in it. Hats this year are small and silly with veils, and Mason has one of those faces that makes you say 'Good gracious, aren't muffins in season now? Do let's have some for tea.' But I told her she looked grand in it. I only hope the poor dear has the right occasion to wear it."

It was because of this conversation that James had his big idea. It was about a week later and Marda had come in to read the paper. He turned to her with broad grin.

"I had an idea in my bath this morning. You know what you told me about Tims and the dogs?"

"Yes."

"Well, I'd thought we'd read up the dogs and pick out some likelies, and then one day soon I'll give the old boy some money and ask him if he'd go racing and back them for me."

Marda was enchanted. James was coming on indeed.

"What a heavenly idea! And I tell you what, couldn't we hint he might take Mason and then she could wear her hat?"

He chuckled.

"Wish I could see them. What shall I say about Mason?"

Marda considered.

"Could you say 'and if Mason could be spared, perhaps you'll take her with you, as she has given long and faithful service' or something like that?"

James was positively giggling.

"It sounds a bit steep, but I could try it."

Marda's eyes shone.

"And I tell you what, we'll kill two birds with one stone. Daisy shall come and wait on you that night."

"Who on earth's Daisy?"

"Your kitchen maid. She comes from the country, and it makes her feel homesick to see flowers, because her mother always has a big bowl on the table and sometimes on the window, too."

"Poor kid!"

Marda sat down and opened the paper.

"She says it wouldn't be so bad if she could get home of a Sunday sometimes, but it's too far. So she just walks about and there's not much to walking alone."

"She's right there."

"It'll be such a good idea if she waits on you. You can lead the subject to gardens, and afterwards you can send for Mrs. Barlow and tell her she's to arrange she gets a long weekend now and again."

He made a face.

"I'd much rather leave Mrs. Barlow to you."

Marda rustled the paper.

"I shall now begin to read. When a man admits he's afraid of his own cook it's time to change the subject."

James was never tired of hearing about Marda's home. Clarice and Edward at school, and what the patients said, and Hannah and her doses, and Alice making two ends meet, and how Harley Street had let them all down by suddenly becoming female and producing kittens called Queen Charlotte and Royal Free, and of how Belisha had been run over and Alistair had given him chloroform and set his leg so that no one would ever know it had been broken.

On one of their walks she told him of Alistair's descent from being a specialist to a G.P. and panel doctor, and about the death of Timothy which had caused it. At the end he was silent so long she was afraid she had bored him.

"I'm sorry I have been talking such a lot."

He did not answer even then for a moment, but he held the hand, which was through his arm to guide him, closer to his side.

"The things you tell me of your family help to explain you."

"How d'you mean?"

He looked as if he were going to speak, then he shook his head.

"Never mind."

About a week later James had his interview with Tims on the subject of the dogs. It was a great success. James, pleased as a schoolboy who has worked a good joke on a master, was waiting for Marda when she came in with the papers.

"Tims thinks that Saturday is the night, as Billy the Bowler is a certainty and nobody knows about him except Tims and the butler next door."

"How did you start the subject?"

"I said, 'Do you know anything about the dogs, Tims?' just like that. To begin with, Tims pretended he didn't know what I was talking about, but after a time he weakened. He's not often been racing, but I gather he usually has a bit on. He'll be delighted to go, purely on my behalf, next Saturday, and he shouldn't wonder if he could bring me home a nice little bit."

"And what about Mason?"

"I failed there. I tried to mention her, but I simply didn't know where to start. I'm afraid you'll have to tackle that."

Marda did tackle Tims that afternoon. He had just finished clearing her lunch.

"I say, Tims, Mr. Longford tells me you know something good for the dogs on Saturday. If I gave you a shilling, would you put it on for me?"

Tims carefully closed the door and came to Marda with a conspiratorial air.

"I'm not talking about him, Miss. If you know a good thing like that, it's as well to keep it quiet. Might pick up a wonderful bit on the tote." He put down his tray and raised his hand and whispered behind it, "But the name is Billy the Bowler, and I think I can say yours'll be a shilling well laid out."

Marda looked suitably grateful.

"That's kind of you." She hesitated and gave him what she hoped was a knowing look. "And I'm sure you won't be going alone?"

Tims was charmed; there was an Edwardian flavour to her suggestion exactly to his mind. He was going alone because the butler next door could not get off on Saturday, but that she should take it for granted he would have a lady with him he found, nevertheless, elevating to his vanity. His face became slightly roguish; if he had been wearing a hat he would have pushed it at a slant.

"Well, I must say having a lady with you does add to an evening, Miss. It gives a bouquet to it, if I may so express myself. But, as a matter of fact, on Saturday I shall be alone."

Marda managed to sound distressed.

"Oh, what a shame!" She paused while allowing the birth of an idea to show on her face. "Oh, Tims, if I arranged that she could have the night off, why don't you take Mason? I have always thought she had rather a soft corner for you."

Tims had been looking less like a bulb grown in the dark lately, but now he actually flushed, a real rosy pink.

"Well—well, I don't know what to say. Of course Ada Mason and I have worked together a long time."

"Shall I see if Mr. Longford could spare her?"

Tims wrestled with his embarrassment, but the thought of a Mason who had been silently worshipping him for years won the day.

"If Mr. Longford allowed it, that would, make the evening very pleasant. Very pleasant indeed."

Saturday evening found Marda, Shirley, and James in James' sitting-room.

"Now, Shirley," Marda begged, "do be sure they're not watching you. Promise you won't let them see you."

James put his arm round Shirley.

"But mind you don't miss anything, Minx. Tell me how the hat looks and if Tims holds her arm."

Shirley gave him a kiss.

"Trust me. Now get back from the window you two."

There was a small veranda. Shirley had already opened the window at the bottom, now she wriggled forward and carefully peered through the wrought-iron edging.

"Can you see the area steps?" Marda asked.

Shirley nodded.

"Yes, got a grand view." There was a moment's pause, then she gave a kick with her heels. "Ssh! They're coming."

James leant over the arm of his chair and found one of Shirley's legs and gave it a pinch.

"Go on, tell us what's happening."

Shirley made a furious face over her shoulders.

"Ssh! They'll hear." She looked at Marda. "She's got on the hat." She went back to her watching, then she turned again. "Tims is looking swell. He's got on a blue suit."

James grinned.

"That'll be one of mine that I've given him. It must be miles too big."

"Oh!" Shirley made a convulsive movement. "She's taken his arm. They're going up the sidewalk."

Marda crept forward.

"Dare I look now, Shirley?"

"Well, keep behind the curtain."

Marda slipped into place. After a moment she gave a pull at James' sleeve.

"Mason's got on a green coat and skirt."

"They're crossing the road," said Shirley. "There! They're out of sight." She wriggled back into the room and sat on the arm of James' chair. "My, I hope they have a swell evening."

Marda looked at the sky.

"I hope it doesn't rain on the hat. It looks very black; I shouldn't wonder if we had a storm."

Shirley leant against James.

"I'm going out tonight. No rummy for you, Jimmie." James looked in Marda's direction.

"Are you going too?"

"Yes. I'm going home and Shirley's going out with some of her queer art students."

Shirley looked at her watch.

"I guess I'd better go and change."

"What are you going to wear?" Marda asked. "I shouldn't think they dress much, do they?"

Shirley's face at once took on the pensive considering look it always wore when her clothes were under discussion.

"Well, I thought that black with the fringed scarf. I guess that'll get them."

James hugged her to him.

"Do you want to get any particular one, Minx?"

Shirley giggled.

"I'll say not. You never saw anything like them. They all look cissie to me. But it's kind of fun going around with them. They never knew anything like me before."

Marda gave her an amused glance.

"I expect that's true." She turned to James. "They paint her all day long. I don't think she ever does any work herself."

Shirley got up.

"You never saw such pictures. Sometimes my face is green, and sometimes it's only half a face, and one of them did me yesterday with a snake coming right out of my ear. 'My,' I said, 'where did you get that notion?' but he said he figured I looked that way. Are you coming, Marda?"

Marda shook her head.

"It's a bit early for me. I'm not dressing up in black crêpe-de-chine with fringed scarves."

"Then stay a bit," said James.

Shirley looked from him to Marda.

"But I wanted Marda to help me dress. Mason's out."

James did not seem to hear the note in Shirley's voice which was so apparent to Marda.

"Well, get this Daisy I've got to talk to."

Shirley stood irresolutely in the middle of the room. She seldom did not get her own way, and failing to threw her all out of gear.

"Oh, very well," she agreed, crossly, "but I think you're pretty mean."

James looked in an amused way towards the door which had slammed after Shirley. His voice was affectionate.

"Spoilt little thing, isn't she?"

Marda was still by the window, watching the storm clouds pile up.

"Yes, but full of character."

James nodded.

"She can't do anything wrong in my eyes. I've got such a lot to thank her for."

Marda turned.

"You mean things have been so different since she came into the house?"

His voice was tender.

"Because of her coming here I've found happiness."

Marda did not move. Until that minute she had not realised how much she had hoped. She had stood out of the way for Shirley, but she had always subconsciously disbelieved that there was any feeling in him for the child, beyond that of guardian. She had been forced to recognise, on the other hand, the real wordless understanding that she, Marda, and he had of each other. And now, in one sentence, he sent all these half-formed hopes toppling. The silence grew so long that it became embarrassing; to break it and to help herself, she moved to the wall and turned on the light which lit the lamp on the table at James' elbow.

James turned his head and gave it a shake.

"Have you turned the lights on?"

"Yes. How did you know? Did you hear the switch?"

"No. There was a lighting of the blackness. For a moment it was grey. It's gone now."

Marda forgot all about herself and her feelings. Her heart was pumping, but the excitement was for him. But she managed to keep her voice casual. It was not right to light a ray of hope in him that might prove to be based on nothing.

"Do you often get that? I mean varying degrees of darkness?"

"No. I don't think so. Lately, when Tims has drawn back my curtains I've thought I did, but I expect I imagine it. I expect I imagined the light just now. I dare say, without being conscious of it, I heard the switch."

Marda came over to the table. The lamp had a switch on itself, a quiet-moving ebonite affair. Her fingers fastened on this and began to ease it through. A distant roll of thunder helped her.

"I shouldn't wonder if there was an awful storm."

"That'll upset the wireless. A bit of a bore with you two out."

She was so absorbed in the light that she had no time to marvel at the change of heart shown in that speech.

"I dare say it won't last long." The switch was through and the light went out.

James once more gave his head a shake.

"Is the light still on?"

Marda decided to lie.

"Yes."

"Well, that settles it. I do imagine things. I could have sworn that the room was darker."

There was a crash of thunder followed by a flame of lightning. Marda had an idea.

"Try the wireless now and see if there is much atmospherics."

The wireless stood against the wall under the far window. James felt his way to it and turned it on. There came another violent crash and, simultaneously, a blinding flash. James blinked.

"Was that lightning?"

Marda had all she could do to steady her voice.

"Just a bit. But the storm's passing."

Marda and Alistair sat in Doctor Ewart's study.

"The trouble is," Doctor Ewart explained to Alistair, "I haven't had a chance to examine him."

"But couldn't you come round now as a friend and see if he'd let you?" Marda begged.

Doctor Ewart leaned towards her.

"I don't know, my dear, how much you understand of the possibilities of what you learnt tonight. You see, Longford was badly concussed and that was followed by blindness. I've always thought the nerves of his eyes were crushed. But, following what you've told us, it might be that there's pressure. Possibly an operation might be worth trying."

"But of course it's worth trying."

Doctor Ewart shook his head.

"It's not going to be as easy as all that. To begin with, if there is even a ray of hope, he ought to see the finest eye surgeon we can lay hands on. It's no good my messing about and getting him X-rayed; that won't get us anywhere."

"Well, who is the finest eye surgeon?"

Doctor Ewart looked at Alistair.

"Mannheim, I suppose."

"Yes; but his clinic's in Switzerland."

Doctor Ewart nodded.

"I know; but he's coming over next month. He's giving a lecture."

Marda clasped her hands.

"Then he'll have to see him. You must make him."

Doctor Ewart gave Alistair an amused glance.

"This daughter of yours will have us moving mountains." He turned back to Marda. "No; if it's done at all, it's a case of we'll have to make him."

Marda accepted that.

"Very well. When will you come and see him?"

Doctor Ewart looked in his book.

"I'll drop in to tea on Sunday afternoon. How's that?"

Marda remembered that Shirley would be out.

"That'll be grand."

Alistair puffed at his pipe and looked at Doctor Ewart.

"Can Mannheim work over here?"

"Yes. Took a degree at Dublin." He threw a glance at Marda. "This young woman of yours seems to have worked marvels with Longford. She told me the first time she saw me that she would, and evidently she's done it."

Marda was brought with a bound to things she had put to the back of her mind. Unknowingly, her face clouded.

"It's not me really, it's Shirley, the girl I was engaged to look after."

Alistair gave her a quick glance.

"I expect you've done your share." He got up. "Come along, my child; you look tired. I'll see you back to Thurloe Square."

In the kitchen, Daisy found Mrs. Barlow.

"I didn't start the talk, honest I didn't. He said to me, 'Where do you come from, Daisy?' just like that."

Mrs. Barlow sniffed.

"You could have kept your place and answered short; there was no reason to go telling him all about your mother, was there?"

"No. But he was so kind, and seemed interested."

Mrs. Barlow's eyes snapped.

"That's what you say, but it's my belief you went whining to him about never getting home."

"Oh no, Mrs. Barlow. I wouldn't do a thing like that."

"Well, it's very queer to me. You meet him for the first time, and the next thing we know is I'm sent for and you're to have a weekend off. It's a nice thing, Tims and Mason tonight, you next weekend. How I'm to carry on nobody tells me. It's my belief he never thought of this on his own. Did you ever talk to Miss Mayne about your home?"

Daisy was no liar.

"Oh, no. Well—I mean—"

Mrs. Barlow sat down and made a majestic gesture to another chair.

"Sit down, Daisy Boundy. We're coming to the truth at last. And when you've told me the truth you can go up and put on your hat, for you're going out to post a letter. I'm writing to Mrs. Cross this very night."

CHAPTER NINE

"DOCTOR Ewart, sir," Tims announced.

James looked towards Marda, who had been reading a thriller to him.

"You know him, of course. Haven't seen him since he sent you to me. Show him in, Tims."

Marda closed her book and got up.

"I'll leave you, then."

"No, don't. Stay and pour out tea for us."

Doctor Ewart came in and shook hands with James. He greeted Marda as if it were not last evening but weeks since they two had met.

"Hullo, my dear! How are you getting on? Is she looking after your ward properly, Longford?"

James smiled.

"She looks after us all. I wish Shirley was in; I'd like you to see her. I gather she's a regular knockout for looks."

Doctor Ewart sat down.

"What is she? Fair, dark?"

"Dark. Exact opposite to Marda here. Regular set of Cochran's Young Ladies I've got."

Marda felt Doctor Ewart's surprised eyes on her. She wanted to say 'All right, don't look at me like that. I know my hair is mid-mouse, and my face, to put it mildly, is homely, but it's not my fault. I never pretended I looked like a Cochran girl.' But somehow she couldn't. James did not care one way or the other how she looked, so what did it matter? All the same, she supposed Doctor Ewart was despising her for deceiving a blind man, and was sorry. She hurriedly took the conversation away from looks.

"We all made money on the dogs last night."

James chuckled.

"My butler knew of a beast called Billy the Bowler that was bound to win. But when he got there the dog was scratched. So he changed over and put all our money on a lady called Ada. It was a compliment, I think, to my housemaid, who went with him. A very lucky compliment as it turned out, for the lady romped home and paid ten to one."

Doctor Ewart was examining James with amazement. He could hardly believe this was the same man he had been visiting for the last six years. There was animation in his voice and eagerness on his face.

"You're looking a lot better. Wonderful what a win on the dogs will do for one."

Tims came in with the tea tray. James heard the sound.

"Put the table by Miss Mayne, Tims. She's pouring out for us. I've just been telling the doctor about your win for us last night. He says it's done me good."

Tims put down his tray and unfolded the tea table and put it in front of Marda.

"The doctor hasn't seen you for some time, sir. I expect he sees a great difference. It's living differently that's done it."

James nodded.

"That's having a ward descend on me, Ewart. I can't call my soul my own. Wireless all day, cards in the evening—"

Marda smoothed the already smooth tea table cloth that Tims had just laid. She must not let herself feel hurt; that way jealousy started again, and jealousy dimmed a person's mentality, and she could not afford to be anything but at her best just now, when all James' chances would hang on her own and Doctor Ewart's powers of persuasion and tact.

Tea over and the door shut on Tims, Doctor Ewart drew up a chair facing James'. His tone was apologetic.

"Do you mind if I pull that curtain across? The sun's in my eyes."

Marda took the hint.

"Let me."

Doctor Ewart thanked her and turned back to James, distracting him from noticing that Marda had pulled the curtains together of one window and the blind down of the other, effectively darkening the room.

"Have you heard about this boy someone's discovered in a Lancashire boxing-booth? He's only sixteen, but he seems remarkable. There was an article about him the other morning.

Seems a natural boxer. Wonderful footwork." As he spoke, he had taken a powerful torch out of his pocket with a reflector attached, and was throwing the light on James' eyes. James blinked and shook his head.

"Yes. Marda read to me about that boy the other morning. Evidently got a find there." He turned his head away from the light.

"Is that light bothering you?" The doctor turned to Marda. "Pull the curtain a little more; it's reflecting off that mirror."

Marda read that aright, and while the doctor put away his torch, she drew back the curtains. Doctor Ewart gave her a look as much as to say, "This is where we plunge. Stand by."

"Do you always feel light like that?"

James stretched out his hand and found the box of cigarettes on the table beside him.

"Smoke?"

The doctor took one and lit it.

"I mean that bothered you, didn't it?"

James lit his cigarette.

"Yes. Has a bit lately. I suppose it's getting out, glare and that. I ought to wear dark glasses, I dare say."

"Who looked after you at the time of your accident?"

"Andrew Brown. Poor old boy, died soon after. Supposed to be a wizard with eyes, but he couldn't do anything for me."

"Told you it was hopeless?"

"More or less. Said I should come back and see him in three months, but I knew that was just to keep my pecker up. He didn't believe himself that he could do anything. Apparently I finished off the nerves, and you can't do anything about that."

The doctor smoked a moment in silence, thinking of the best way to put his case.

"You should have gone back to Brown, though."

"I should have had a long trip. He was dead before the three months were up."

"Well, then, you should have gone to somebody else."

James was growing restive. Marda saw the well-known signs that his nerves were getting frayed.

"Rot! I hate being messed about."

"Even if there was a chance of saving all, or part, of your sight?"

James's unseeing eyes were fixed on the doctor.

"That's impossible. The nerves were killed."

"I'm not so sure. Dead nerves can't react to light; yours do."

James's hands were twitching.

"I dare say I imagine it."

Marda thought it was time she joined in.

"I don't believe you do. You noticed the light turned on the other night, and you told me you thought you knew when Tims drew back the curtains in the mornings."

Doctor Ewart backed her.

"Seems common sense that you should see somebody."

James shrank back into his chair.

"All that messing about for one chance in ten million. Not me."

"There needn't be much messing about. Just an X-ray. If that shows nothing can be done, they'll tell you. An X-ray doesn't take long."

Marcia looked at him.

"If he did let somebody see him, who's the best person to do it?"

The doctor pretended to consider.

"A fellow called Mannheim. A Swiss."

James exploded.

"If you think I'm going to be dragged half across Europe to see some fellow who can't do me any good, you're mistaken."

The doctor smoked placidly.

"Naturally, you won't go to Switzerland; but I have an idea Mannheim will be over next month. He's lecturing or something. Any case he's over here off and on. He has a Dublin degree."

"I don't care if he comes and lives in this street. I'm not going to see him. I know I'm blind, and I don't need anybody to tell me they can't cure me."

Marda gave the doctor a despairing look, but he replied with a reassuring nod.

"Oh, well, there's no hurry," he said cheerfully. "Mannheim won't be here for a month. Tell me, you're fairly knowledge-able, what will it cost to train a boy like this Lancashire boxer?"

On the excuse that boxing was not her subject, Marda left the room. She waited in Shirley's sitting-room for the doctor to come down. But evidently boxing proved an engrossing subject, for before he appeared, Shirley came back from her tea party.

"Hullo!" Her voice was pleased. "Sitting down here?"

"Doctor Ewart, a friend of Mr. Longford's, turned up to tea."

Shirley's face became alert.

"Is he still there?"

"Yes. If you're going to let him see you, you'd better spread on the glamour; he's had a very dazzling description of you."

Shirley hung over Marda's chair.

"From Uncle Jimmie? What did he say?"

"That you looked like one of Cochran's Young Ladies."

Shirley went to the glass and repowdered her nose and made up her mouth.

"I guess he ought to see me, then. I'm not that type."

"They're all types. I dare say if you had leanings in that direction, Mr. Cochran would consider you."

Shirley put her make-up back in her bag.

"Nuts on that. Too much competition on the stage." She raised her innocent Madonna eyes. "I'd say I look just right to vamp a doctor."

Marda, eyeing the clock, decided Shirley was right. It was a good quarter of an hour after she went up that she heard the doctor on the stairs. She went out to meet him, and he grinned.

"That child you're bear-leading is a card." He tucked a hand under Marda's arm. "Can young ladies walk bareheaded up the square?"

Outside Marda said:

"You see how it is?"

He nodded.

"It's going to be hard work, but you'll manage it. Get that little charmer upstairs to help you."

Marda was ashamed of herself, but that crushed her a little. It would have been warming if he had just said, 'You'll manage it.' It was maddening, but true, Shirley was the person who could help. They walked on a little way in silence, and then she said:

"What about Mrs. Cross? If you wrote to her, wouldn't that be a help? After all, she's his sister."

They were at the corner and stopped automatically.

"Mrs. Cross is a very maternal woman." He was obviously feeling for his words. "She has let her boy and his welfare absorb her."

"But surely in a matter like this she'd make an effort? I mean anyone would, even a stranger. I wonder she hasn't done it before. She must have known he was supposed to go back and see his surgeon in three months."

He patted her arm.

"You're a very straightforward, straight-thinking person, my dear, and it's difficult for you to grasp the twists there might be in another person's mind. You see right and wrong quite clearly. It's not so easy for everybody else."

Marda looked up at him in puzzlement.

"But could there be any question of right or wrong about this? Here's a man convinced he is blind for life, and got a phobia about being examined, or even having his eyes discussed. Surely even if there's one chance in a million for his sight to come back, it must be right to force him to give himself a chance?"

He patted her arm again.

"I know. But trust me, and don't ask any questions when I say Mrs. Cross is better out of this. Goodnight, my dear."

Marda had a talk with Shirley that night. Shirley was undressing and Marda sat on the end of her bed.

"Doctor Ewart didn't come here simply as a social call. I asked him to. I've seen signs lately that Mr. Longford isn't stone blind. I wanted to see if I was right."

Shirley was brushing her hair. She swung round on her dressing-table stool.

"What did he say?"

"He thinks there's a chance. He wants him to see a man called Mannheim who'll be in this country next month."

"My!" Shirley hugged her brush to her in ecstasy. "Isn't that just wonderful! But why didn't he say anything tonight? Sat there all the evening just as though nothing had happened."

"From his point of view nothing has. He doesn't believe it. He says he won't let Mannheim look at him, nor anyone else."

"Gosh! Is he plumb crazy?"

Marda curled up on the bed.

"No, it's a phobia. He doesn't like his eyes talked about, and won't have them looked at."

"But why?"

Marda pleated the eiderdown.

"I think it's natural, if you think it out. It's all part of the way he's put up with the whole business. You know, shutting himself up and not seeing his friends, being afraid of being pitied. You know, he must have gone through a ghastly time at the beginning, and probably the memory of it still turns him sick when he thinks of it. It's like somebody who's been buried in an earthquake, can't stand a roof over their head. It's a kind of recurrent fear. That's how it is with him. He's been through that awful time and he revolts at the thought of even a torch on his eyes."

"But if there's a chance he might see?"

"He doesn't believe it for a moment. He found himself blinded and has accepted that fact just as one accepts one has ten toes."

Shirley took off her dressing-gown and wandered over to the bed to fetch her nightdress. Marda, in spite of being engrossed in what she was saying, took her in. The brief pink chiffon camiknickers she had on showed every line of her figure. If James were really to see again, how much more lovely he would find her even than he had imagined!

Shirley pulled a white chiffon nightdress, tied with blue satin ribbons, over her head.

"If he feels like that, how are we going to make him feel differently? Jimmie's so stubborn. Look at the weeks it took to even get a radio into his room."

"I thought perhaps if you talked to him and asked him to see Mannheim to please you, he might give in. You'll have to choose your moment, of course, but I think that's the best chance."

Shirley threw her camiknickers across the room and got into bed.

"Is this an act?"

Marda looked at her in surprise.

"What d'you mean?"

"All this talk about me persuading. What's the matter with you? Tongue rotted on you?"

"Don't be such an idiot. He's fond of you and might give in just to please you."

"I suppose he fairly hates you." Suddenly Shirley bounced out of bed and threw her arms round Marda. "All right, you prize fool, I'll talk to him, and then you can talk after that. We'll have a lot of liqueurs with our coffee one night and get him so mellow he doesn't know if he's saying 'yes' or 'no.'"

Marda kissed her.

"Goodnight, darling. I'll leave it to you. I know you have great faith in drink."

Shirley got back into bed and leant against her pillows.

"Did you ever get around to studying ostriches?"

Marda was at the door; she turned.

"Ostriches! No. Only that they're supposed to bury their heads in the sand. Why?"

"That's why." Shirley yawned and lay down. "Goodnight."

Seeing Doctor Ewart seemed to have made James nervous. During the next few days he had to be handled with care. Any suggestion of a departure from routine scared him.

"I guess we'll have to leave the drinking evening for a bit," Shirley told Marda. "I reckon by the end of the week he'll have settled down."

Marda woke on the Thursday to find one of those clear days of brilliant sunshine which belong to early autumn.

"This is the day," she thought to herself, "to get him back to normal. A nice brisk walk in the Park ought to do anybody good." Thinking these things, she went upstairs after breakfast with the papers under her arm, whistling as she went.

The morning did seem to have done James good. He looked more rested and less nervous and he greeted Marda with a pleased smile.

"Hullo! I have been hanging out of the window. It's a grand day, isn't it?"

"Marvellous! I thought I'd get through the papers quickly and we'd go out early."

He fumbled on his table and produced a letter. "Would you read this to me? Tims tells me it's from my sister."

Marda took the envelope from him and sat down. The words "From Mrs. Cross, The Old Windmill, Exedown, Devon," were written on the flap. Marda was afraid to open the envelope. She never remembered a sensation like that before. The words and hints of so many people ran through her mind. Mason's in answer to her "But Mrs. Cross, doesn't she get him out?" Her obvious hesitancy and then, "No, Miss." Daisy's "If you ask me, she is coming to see how he is. She's got no money. He's got it all, and she's watching to see nobody gets hold of any of it. She wants it all put by for Master Edward." And finally, Doctor Ewart's "Trust me and don't ask any questions when I say Mrs. Cross is better out of this." Unwillingly, she put her finger under the flap and tore it open.

My Dear Jim,

How are you? I feel such a wicked sister not having been to see you for so long. So now I mean to make up for all that and pay you a lovely long visit. Eddie sends you such a lot of love and says he would simply 'ove to see 'oo himself, but he has had such a nasty time with his tumtum Mummie says he mustn't.

I shall arrive on Saturday, if you will tell Mason to have my room ready. I will send you a telegram to say by what train, and perhaps you will send Tims in a taxi to meet me, as I have always been such a silly little person about luggage, have not I?

Much love from your affectionate sister,

VERA.

There was a silence as Marda finished the letter and folded it up and put it back in its envelope. Marda did not care for the letter at all, but obviously could not say so, and what James felt he kept to himself. After a moment or two, he said in rather a depressed voice:

"Well, that's that! Will you tell Tims and Mason?"

"Shall I read now?" Marda asked, opening the paper. James did not answer, so she repeated her question. He came back to the present with a jump.

"Sorry! I was miles away. What did you say?"

"Only asked if I should read." He nodded.

Marda read for nearly an hour, political news, society news, sports news. She left out nothing.

During the whole time she was conscious that James never heard a word. With a troubled face he sat limply in his chair, gazing into space.

Marda folded the paper and opened her mouth to say, "Shall we go out now?" Then she closed it again. She and James were not the best company for each other this morning. Reading out loud, she was able not to worry consciously, but she was more than aware that with no distraction she would worry. It was bad enough to be uneasy about Mrs. Cross's visit, but now she felt something much stronger than uneasiness. What in the world was there about Mrs. Cross to make her brother troubled because she was going to pay a visit? Would Mrs. Cross be a good influence at this most crucial moment? Would she help to get James to see Mannheim? How would the coming of Mrs. Cross affect herself? Would she be able to see as much of James? Because she was afraid that walking with him in the Park she would be unable to keep Mrs. Cross out of the conversation, and because it was clear James needed distraction, Marda had an idea.

"Would you like to come home with me this morning?" She saw his nervous move and forestalled his objections.

"I don't suppose Mother will be in, and the twins, as you know, are at school, and of course Dad'll be out on his round, but I'd like you to meet Harley Street and Belisha."

Unconsciously Marda's tone was wistful. James reacted at once. He forced his voice to be brighter than he felt.

"Not to mention Queen Charlotte and Royal Free." He smiled. "I'll be proud to meet them. Get Tims to get a taxi."

Alice was in. She was in Edward's bedroom, turning out a cupboard, when the taxi stopped. She leant on the sill and watched James and Marda get out of the taxi, and quite unexpectedly found herself swept back twenty-eight years. She saw herself and Alistair getting out of a taxi. It was odd she should have remembered that day, for as far as she could recall nothing important had happened except that she was almost delirious with happiness at being alone with Alistair. She could even remember how she looked. She had worn a beaver hat trimmed with gold flowers, and a short musquash coat, and she had thought, because Alistair's face so plainly showed that he thought so, that she looked nice. Now she could smile at her young self; how comic her appearance would seem today, with her long skirt, and the high-boned collar of her blouse! Just as quickly as the vision of her past came to her, so it vanished, and she was looking down at James' well-groomed figure, and Marda, slim and attractive, with a blue coat over a wool frock. "I wonder," she marvelled, "why they made me think of Alistair and me? For there's nothing in common. I never helped Alistair; he was always looking after me." Then suddenly she knew where the sameness came in. It was in Marda's face as she looked at James: she was certain that was just how she had looked at Alistair.

Marda raised her head and saw her mother; instead of calling out as she would have done normally, she put a finger on her lips. She knew how James would shrink at the thought that he was being watched, and how nervous he would become if he knew Alice was in. She took him by the arm and led him up the steps, talking casually.

"I'll call Hannah and find out who is in." Harley Street came out from behind the area bars and rubbed herself against James' legs. "That's Harley Street."

James leant down and stroked the cat's back.

"Where are Queen Charlotte and Royal Free?"

That gave Marda the excuse she wanted. She could see Hannah's interested face at the kitchen window. She beckoned to her.

"Good morning, Hannah. This is Mr. Longford. Where are the kittens?"

Hannah came up the area steps.

"Good morning, sir." She turned to Marda. "Out in the scullery. The butcher will take one, and they'd like the other at a house up the street, but I said we'd better keep one to give Harley Street something to give her thoughts to. If she's left with nothing to do she might go out and have another slip."

James laughed.

"How's your parsley? Miss Mayne says you grow it."

"That's right, sir." Hannah, forgetting he could not see, nodded over her shoulder at her pots. "It's finished now, though." She leant against the area rails. "How's Miss Shirley getting on?"

"Splendidly." James smiled. "We're all doing splendidly under Miss Mayne. She runs the entire house."

Hannah gave him an approving look.

"Glad you've got the sense to appreciate your luck. There's only one Miss Marda, and so I've always said."

Marda flushed.

"Don't be silly, Hannah."

"It's true, though." Hannah was never put off saying what she had in mind. "And you agree with me, don't you, sir?"

James laughed, but his voice had a note of sincerity that warmed Marda's heart.

"I do indeed."

Marda moved the conversation off herself.

"Is Mother in? Dad's out, I suppose."

"Your mother's up turning out Edward's cupboard. He kept something nasty there last holidays, and it's smelling fit to beat the band. Mrs. Mayne says it's his moths, but it smells more like a dead bird to me. Your Dad's out: one of the Jams rang up for him this morning; wanted him urgent on account of a pain. He said it wouldn't be anything much, but I said there's no need to take that view till we know; there's many a stomach-ache that finished as an appendix."

James and Marda went into the house laughing.

"She's exactly as you described her," James whispered.

Marda, seeing that Hannah had made him feel at home, risked calling her mother.

"Mum! Mum!"

"Oh, don't bother," James said nervously.

Marda paid no attention to him, but held him firmly by the arm and talked to Alice as she ran down the stairs.

"Darling, I thought it was time Mr. Longford met some of the family."

Alice took James' hand.

"I'm so glad you've come. We've been longing to meet you. We've such a lot to thank you for."

James' voice was honestly surprised.

"To thank me for? I should have thought the shoe was on the other foot."

Alice led the way into the drawing-room.

"Oh no. Apart from Marda's job, which is a Godsend, there's the tennis for the twins, and all the other fun they had with Shirley."

"I hear your Edward fell for my minx of a ward."

Alice settled herself in an armchair facing him and reached to the window ledge for her workbasket.

"Such a good thing. I couldn't have believed he could have been tidied up so quickly. By the end of the holidays he really looked quite well groomed."

Marda sat on the arm of her mother's chair.

"He seems to have reverted to type. Hannah says you've been digging for the body in his bedroom cupboard."

Alice searched the heel of a sock for thin places.

"Dear Edward! I'm sure he must have packed in a rush or he would have remembered."

Marda leant down and pulled another sock out of the mending basket.

"What was it?"

Alice made a face.

"Meat sandwiches. He had them made for lunch one day, and then he lunched with a friend and never used them. They had got very nasty."

Marda had found a hole, so she leant down again and collected some wool and a darning needle.

"He is a dirty hound."

James was leaning back in his chair looking easy and at home. This domestic gossip between Marda and her mother was just right for him; he could have no illusion that his blindness was making for awkwardness. The door opened and Hannah came in.

"Hullo, Hannah," Marda said quickly, knowing James loathed to hear footsteps and not know whose they were.

Hannah made a face to silence Marda, and held out her orders slate. On it was written, "Should I bring up the sherry we had for the trifle?"

Alice turned to James.

"Would you like a glass of sherry? I'm afraid it's not very good."

"I could slip out," Hannah suggested, "and get something that isn't cooking."

James shook his head.

"No, thank you."

Hannah sighed.

"Pity it's not teatime. Seems all wrong you should come and us offer nothing."

James turned his eyes towards where he supposed her to be.

"That's nice of you, but I haven't done anything to deserve the fatted calf."

"That's as may be." Hannah looked across at Marda. "I was down at my sister's yesterday. I picked a sweetly pretty bunch of chrysanths for you."

Marda put down her darning and got up.

"You are an angel. I'll come down and get them."

Left alone with James, Alice could not resist leading him on to praise her daughter.

"I do hope Marda's really useful?"

He was silent a moment, turning over her words with a faintly amused expression on his face.

"Those words seem so inadequate to express all she is. She's made me see that there's still fun in the world, even for a crock like myself."

Alice was too used as a doctor's wife to hearing complaints called by their right names to flinch at words.

"I shouldn't describe a blind man as a crock. Of course it must be ghastly at first, but I should have imagined that other senses grew so acute in time as almost to take the place of not being able to see. Don't you find you get very vivid impressions through your ears? I mean, haven't you got quite a good idea what I'm like from hearing me speak?"

"Yes, I should have had, but I've gone wrong lately. I couldn't have been more out than I was over Marda. From the moment I heard her speak, and she has such a beautiful speaking voice, I had the clearest idea of how she would look. You could, as I'm sure Hannah would say, 'have knocked me down with a feather' when I knew what she really looked like."

"Really? How did you imagine her?"

James considered a moment.

"Not dark or fair, but something between. Those grey eyes that look as if there is always a laugh hanging about somewhere. Not curling hair, but fitting neatly into the crease at the back of her neck like feathers on a duck. Oh, I don't know; a vividness that has nothing to do with pretty-prettyness—anyway quite the opposite to what she is."

Alice had laid down her darning to listen with interest to this accurate piece of mind drawing.

"The opposite? How d'you mean?"

"Well, I hear she's fair, yellow curls, blue eyes, just like an English rose."

Alice's eyes goggled.

"But—"

She was interrupted by Marda, who, holding the bunch of chrysanthemums, came in with Belisha.

"I've brought Belisha to see you." She took the dog by the collar and led him over to James.

James stooped and found Belisha's head and ran his ears through his fingers. He looked up at Marda.

"How good those chrysanthemums smell!"

Marda held the bunch to his nose.

"Yes. Can't you imagine them growing? The last of them in a rather windswept flowerbed, with dead leaves blowing round."

Alice was staring at her so hard that Marda was conscious of her eyes, and flushed. Alice's face was concerned. What was Marda up to? She did not approve of interfering in her children's lives, but deceiving a blind man was a wretched business, and utterly unlike her.

"Mr. Longford and I have just been discussing seeing with the mind." Her voice took on a firm note. "If I were you, Mr. Longford, I wouldn't rely too much on this daughter of mine."

James' face was distressed.

"No. You're right, I mustn't. A man like myself has no right to be dependent on anyone." He got up. "I think we ought to be going."

Marda crossed to her mother and gave her a kiss, but without her usual fervour. What on earth had come over her? she marvelled. She was always so understanding. Couldn't she see how James would read a remark like that?

When they had gone, Alice stood at the window watching the taxi disappear up the street. She tapped an angry little tattoo on the pane. "Bother! I am a silly woman! I said the wrong thing, obviously. But why tell him fairytales?" Her fingers paused in their drumming, and she caught her breath. What did make women do strange things foreign to their natures? "Oh no," she said out loud. "Not that, Marda dear. Don't tie yourself to a blind man."

Shirley came in from her art school and ran upstairs to Marda's room. Marda was tidying a drawer. Shirley put an arm round her waist and pushed a paper under her nose.

"How's that?"

Marda looked where Shirley's finger was pointing, and read, "The Southerners. Tonight at eight-thirty."

"What about them?"

Shirley turned away and sat on Marda's bed, hugging her knees.

"I rang up a ticket agency and booked two seats. You're taking Jimmie."

Marda eyed her in amazement.

"But he wouldn't go. I know he wouldn't. Anyway, why tonight?"

Shirley hugged her knees tighter.

"I wouldn't say Jimmie was a musical man, but I guess I've got him just a mite tickled with spirituals. That's why I thought of it. I suddenly saw the Southerners were giving a concert, and I thought, well, one excuse is as good as another."

Marda sat beside Shirley.

"Why do you want him to go?"

"Just my sweet nature. There's old Mother Cross coming in the morning, and maybe this is the last pleasant evening you'll have for quite a while, so I thought you might as well enjoy it. The thought of seeing his sister has made Jimmie lower than a snake, so I'd say he'd be better taken out and get his mind off her."

Marda played with the coverlet on the bed.

"Well, can't you get out of what you're doing and take him, always provided you can get him to go?"

Shirley twinkled.

"'Tisn't often I let my better nature come uppermost, so don't hold out on me. I'm going to a dance, and this is a little treat planned for you."

Marda laughed.

"It's awfully nice of you, but I'm afraid it's a waste of two tickets. I expect they'll have to be given to Tims and Mason."

Shirley got off the bed and wandered round the room, fidgeting with this and that.

"Don't you ever go right out for a thing? Do you always just sit down and say, 'If it's meant for me it'll fall right here in my lap'?"

Marda was puzzled.

"What are you talking about?"

Shirley gave a chuckle and came over and kissed her.

"I guess you're just plumb crazy. What I was talking about was the concert. Now you go right down to Jimmie and get round him. Say it was your idea, say you wanted to go, say it's your birthday, say you've just lost a relative and need cheering up."

Marda was amused.

"But none of it's true."

Shirley sighed.

"Well, just tell him the truth. Say I bought the tickets, say I suggested you should go; but don't you dare face me, Marda Mayne, if you haven't talked him into it."

James was listening to the wireless when Marda came in. He switched it off and looked towards her.

"Hullo, Marda, what are you up to?"

She sat down on a humpty.

"Shirley wants me to take you to a concert."

"A concert?" James' face was horrified. "But she knows I never go anywhere. I hate being seen in public."

Marda suddenly saw the concert as important. It would be one more step, before his sister arrived, in James' emancipation. If only he could be got to this concert, and enjoyed it, and did not feel self-conscious, it would be another of those little things which would bolster him up in the possibly difficult days to come.

"It's rather a special concert," she explained. "It's those negroes called The Southerners, that Shirley's so keen on. I should think it very unlikely you'd meet anybody you knew, and I do think you'd enjoy hearing them."

James looked scared.

"I'd much rather not. A concert's just the kind of thing at which you do run into people. I've made it quite clear I want to be left alone, and don't want to be looked up, and if I'm seen about, that'll start everybody calling again."

Marda for the moment toyed with the thought of arguing with him on his seclusion fixation, but almost at once she discarded the idea. There was only one subject that was worth arguing about at the moment, and that was his visit to Mannheim. Absolutely nothing else mattered. She let the subject of the concert go.

"Oh, very well, I thought you might say that. It was just that it sounded such a lovely concert."

She was looking at him, and she saw a flush rise over his cheekbones; his voice was full of contrition.

"Oh, my dear, what a selfish hound it makes of one, being a crock! Here am I thinking of nothing but myself. You take the tickets. Can't Shirley go with you?"

"Shirley's going to a dance, and I'm certainly not going to the concert without you. It doesn't matter a bit; we'll stop here, and I'll read you some more of that thriller."

James had a visible struggle with himself, then he said: "Ring for Tims, will you?"

"What d'you want? Can't I get it?"

"You'll see."

Tims came in, and James turned to him.

"Tims, Miss Mayne is making me go to a concert tonight." He looked towards Marda. "What time does it begin?"

"Eight-thirty."

"Tell Mrs. Barlow we'll dine at seven-fifteen, and I'll get into a dinner-jacket." He smiled towards Tims. "That's to say if you can find one that's fit to wear."

Tims looked almost eager.

"Oh yes, sir. There's all your things, as good as ever they were, and there's no alteration in your figure, sir, not to notice. I'll lay them out now." He looked across at Marda. "I'm sure it's a very good idea, Miss Mayne. There's nothing like a bit of music; it puts heart into you."

It was Marda more than James who was nervous as the car stopped at the concert-hall; she slipped her hand through his arm and held him tightly to her. There were such a lot of people going in, and she didn't want him jostled and fussed. She prayed fervently that by no ill chance would they run into anyone that he knew. It would be the most maddeningly ill luck.

Their seats were on a gangway, and Marda piloted James into his without mishap, and bought a programme, and because she was certain that he must be feeling his blindness acutely, wondering who was near him and if he were being stared at, she broke into hurried conversation. She told him about the audience, what was on the programme, of the flowers massed at the side of the platform. He did not seem to take in what she said, for quite suddenly he laid a hand on her knee and ran a piece of the stuff of her frock through his fingers.

"What have you got on?"

"Black. It's what I call my G.B.D. It means a Good Black Dress, and it's a very present help in time of trouble, or perhaps trouble's the wrong word. I should say parties, because being black, people don't notice it much, and nobody says, 'Look, there's Marda, wearing the same frock she wore last year.'"

James pictured Marda's fair curls, and pink-and-white skin, rising out of black.

"Black ought to suit you."

"Oh dear, no. I really look best in green, but it's an extravagant colour, because people remember it."

"Green?" said James in surprise. "Really!" Then his mind reverted to her as she was looking tonight. "I bet a lot of people are staring at you."

She looked round. Not one soul, as far as she could see, was taking the slightest interest in her or James.

"No. Everybody is very sensibly taking an interest in themselves." Then her eye fell on a red-faced man two rows in front of them, who was craning his neck to get a look at James. More to relieve her own mind than his, she said firmly, "Nobody's interested in us at all." Then she touched his arm. "There, the conductor's just come in, and the lights are going out."

The negro choir were massed on the platform. Through the darkened hall their beautifully rounded, weird, tragic, plaintive notes pierced the phlegmatic British audience. It was practically impossible to sit and listen to the choir without unconsciously swaying to their almost intolerable rhythm, which beat through everything that they sang like notes on a tom-tom. Marda was entranced. She knew that a large part of her happiness was in being with James, but as well, because she was carried out of herself by the music, she was able for a little while to believe that dreams could come true, that some day the position between herself and James would be altered, that he'd love her as she loved him. The first half of the programme finished with the triumphant "All God's chillun got shoes." As the applause died away, Marda turned glowingly to James.

"Wasn't that lovely?"

"Yes." He shrank into his seat. "What's happening? What's everybody moving about for?"

"It's the interval. They're going out for a smoke. Do you want to?"

"Good God, no."

It was then that Marda saw the man who had been staring at James before the concert started. He had got up in his seat and, marking James down, was plainly coming to speak to him. She held her breath, and sent up an unconscious prayer to heaven: "Don't let that man stop and speak. Please let him go outside and forget about us."

Her prayer was unanswered. The man bore straight down, stopped by James' seat, and held out his hand.

"Why, Jim, you old son of a gun, where've you been hiding? I haven't heard of you since we did that cricket tour." He gave his hand an expectant shake. "Come on, old man, you're not going to tell me you've forgotten me. I know I've buried myself in Assam, but I'm still the same Victor Greg."

Marda saw the tragedy that was coming. The outstretched hand of Victor, that James could not see. Quick as lightning she opened her bag, and as she had no pencil, took out her lipstick and wrote on the back of her programme, "B L I N D," and held it in front of Victor.

Victor reacted quicker than Marda could have hoped. In one second he had dropped his hand, and was shaking Jim's, and at the same time had burst into a flood of reminiscence.

Did Jim remember old Podger? He'd run into him somewhere in Bangkok. Had he heard that the Walrus had married the most lovely girl, and everybody supposed he must have done it by hypnotism, because after all the Walrus had never been much to look at, had he! In the middle of this flood James came suddenly to himself.

"I say, you must think me awfully rude. This is Miss Mayne. She's being bear-leader to my ward."

Victor shook Marda's hand. She smiled up at him gratefully.

"Bear-leading is the word. His ward is seventeen, and she was brought up in America."

Victor seemed to find that very funny.

"You've never got a seventeen-year-old girl as a ward, have you? Shouldn't have thought they'd have trusted you with her." He turned back to Marda. "Jim here and I were at Oxford together. I could tell you some stories about him then."

James made an effort. He was so unused to meeting his friends that the exchange of ordinary conversation came hard to him.

"Shirley, my ward, is the daughter of Don Kay. You remember him."

"Poor old Don! I read in a paper he'd gone. Died in New York, didn't he?"

James was easier.

"Yes. His wife died when the child was born. Did you ever see her? He married before he went down."

"No, I never met her. Bit of a beauty, wasn't she?"

"So's the daughter," said James. "Beautifully made, and lovely colouring."

Victor looked at him with rounded eyes.

"She can't have been with you long. He only died this year."

"That's right," James agreed.

Marda saw that the unconscious way in which James handed on her own description of Shirley had completely flummoxed Victor. He was obviously anxious now to get away, so she tried to help him.

"I'm looking forward to the next half of the programme, aren't you? Look, the orchestra's coming back. It oughtn't to be long."

"No, by Jove," said Victor. "Must just go outside for a snifter of air." He leant down and patted James' shoulder. "Well, so long, old man. I'm stopping at my club; if you sent me a line there you'd get me. I'd enjoy a yarn."

Marda and James sat in silence for a moment or two after Victor had gone, then Marda said as casually as though James met friends every day:

"Funny running into him like that."

He turned towards her.

"D'you know I don't believe he could have known about me. I never knew him well. D'you think it's possible he thought I could see?"

Marda with her handkerchief rubbed her lipstick-drawn letters off the back of the programme.

"I don't see why not. After all, you don't look different."

James was suddenly at ease. He turned his head as though he could see round the hall.

"I dare say he didn't get on to how things are. As you say, I don't look any different." The conductor came back, and rapped on his stand. James lay back in his seat, found Marda's hand and ran his fingers through hers. "I'm enjoying myself," he said happily. "We must do this again."

CHAPTER TEN

THE whole house waited for Mrs. Cross, and heard the front-door bell ring. "That'll be Tims and 'Her,'" said Mason, gloomily, as she got up to let them in.

Daisy, washing up the tea-things in the scullery, stopped what she was doing and bit the back of her hand, a habit she always found helpful in times of emotion.

"Oh, I hope 'She' doesn't stay long. Mother and Dad will be so upset me not coming for the weekend after me writing to say I could and all. But Miss Mayne said she'd see I had the very next after 'She's' gone, and she's not one that would break a promise."

"That'll be your sister," said Marda, closing the thriller she was reading to James. "I'll just have one more look at the bedroom. I do hope she'll like it. It's a pity I am in the one she has always used. I wouldn't have minded moving, you know."

James was looking strained.

"I wouldn't hear of it. The room was redecorated for you."

Shirley had been watching out of the window for the taxi. As it stopped at the door she took one more glance at herself in the mirror and went down the stairs. As she walked her eyes twinkled, and she gave a pleased pat to the skirt of her new grey angora frock.

Vera Cross was a woman who built her life round things she imagined. She imagined she had been heartbroken at the death of her husband, and had been living as a heartbroken widow ever since. Actually, her husband had been a bad-tempered man who was idiotic about money and she had been far happier without him. She imagined she was rather a pathetic little figure, and behaved as she thought pathetic little figures should behave. Actually, she was a stout, flabby woman, who scared people by the indomitable purpose in her eye. She knew herself to be a good woman, and would have been horrified if she had known that muddled thinking was taking her so far from charity that all that was good in her nature was rotting.

One of her strongest imaginings was that pathetic, heart-broken widows hated travelling. In reality she rather enjoyed journeys; there was always a chance she might find some unfortunate in the carriage who had not the courage to move into the corridor, to whom she could tell her version of her life-history and the latest stories of her little Edward. Now in the hall of Thurloe Square she was giving Tims and Mason a very good display of how pathetic widows behave after long journeys.

"Take my cases straight up, Mason. If I can squeeze a teeny minute before dinner, I should like a weeny rest. I'm afraid I've never quite got used to travelling alone, and it makes me very tired."

It was at this moment that Shirley appeared on the bend of the stairs. Vera gave a tremendous start.

"Who is this, Tims?"

Tims swallowed preparatory to answering, but Shirley saved him the trouble.

"Don't you remember me? I'm Shirley Kay."

Vera expressed enlightenment.

"Of course. But you were a child when I last saw you. Have you been kind and looking up my poor, poor Jim?"

"Yep. Do nothing but look him up. I live here, you know."

Vera gave Shirley what she hoped was a sweet glance, but was in fact one which bristled with malice.

"Really! No, I hadn't been told."

"I suppose you haven't," Shirley agreed, pleasantly. "Being blind, poor Jimmie can't write letters, can he? But we are delighted to have you. I've been saying to him for weeks, 'Do ask your sister here; I'm sure we ought.'"

Vera, conscious of very peculiar in-drawings of breath from Mason, and of Tims, who, though silent, must be thinking a lot, bit back all the snappy retorts she would like to have made. She came forward and patted Shirley kindly on the shoulder.

"Funny little girl. Well, I must go up and see my brother. We must have what my little boy calls 'a cosy' later. He means a cosy talk, you know."

Shirley nodded.

"You bet we will."

With great dignity Vera mounted the stairs. She forgot to be a tired little widow, and instead looked what she was, a strong woman out for vengeance. Shirley waited until she was round the corner, and then gave Tims and Mason an enormous wink.

"Carry the bags up, Mason. I think she'll need more than a weeny rest." She then bounded up the stairs to Marda, who was in her bedroom, and flung herself down on the bed. "She's come, darling."

Marda sat down beside her.

"What's she like?"

Shirley considered.

"Well, I'd say outwardly she was like a cow suffering from flatulence, but inside I guess a couple of knives have nothing on her."

"Was it an awful shock to her to see you?"

Shirley sat up and hugged her knees.

"That's the interesting part. She gave a grand performance of a woman suffering from shock, but she was expecting to find me here, and you too, I guess."

Marda frowned.

"But how could she? Mr. Longford didn't write, he told me so."

Shirley narrowed her eyes.

"Let's work this thing out. There's Doctor Ewart. Would he tell her?"

"No; he didn't want her to know. He wasn't sure that she would be the right person to persuade him to go to Mannheim."

Shirley gave a sudden bounce.

"I have it. I know where the body's buried. It will be Mrs. Barlow. She's mad as a hornet at my being here, your being here, and the meals being different, Mason and Tims going to the dogs, and Daisy having a weekend. She's been in this house since the days of Oliver Cromwell, and she doesn't want anything altered. I bet you she wrote."

Marda was unwilling to believe stories of anybody, but she could see that Shirley's reasoning was probably right.

"Perhaps she thought it her duty. Perhaps she thinks we're not good for Mr. Longford."

"Oh, yeh?" Shirley got up. "Well, if you're going to be the charitable angel, I'm not. That Vera and I are just a couple of girls without a thought in common, and she is going to get out of this house in double-quick time, or I'm not as tough as I thought."

Vera had pulled herself together at James' door, and it was the pathetic little widow who kissed him on both cheeks.

"How is little brother? An elder sister has been a naughty woman to neglect him so long."

James bore with her kisses, but hurried to find her a chair.

"How are you, my dear? How's the boy?"

"Not very strong. I've got a lot of things to talk about, and he's one of them. Why didn't you tell me you had Shirley Kay here? Of course it mustn't go on for another day; it's not suitable at all. I must take the girl back to Devonshire with me."

A faint amusement covered James' face at the picture of Shirley in Devonshire with Vera.

"Oh, I've got the child a chaperone. As a matter of fact, I like having her here—she brightens me up. You'd hardly know me."

"I don't see any signs of brightening. As I came into the room I said to myself, 'Oh, my poor Jim, what have you been doing? You do look wretched.'"

James ran a hand over his face.

"Don't know how I look, but I know how I feel."

Vera took off her gloves.

"What sort of creature is the chaperone? Old, I hope, and sensible. That child plainly needs a lot of looking after. Of course I know I'm only a sister, and not very strong, and you probably think have more than enough troubles of my own, but you should have wired for me. I would gladly have stayed in the house as long as the child is here."

James lit a cigarette.

"The child is here for good, or at least until she marries. Don died in America and left me her guardian."

"For good!" Vera could not keep the dismay out of her voice. Mrs. Barlow's letter had not suggested anything as bad as this. For the last six years James' house and his servants had been hers to command. She did not come up much in the summer, but throughout the winter she treated the house like an hotel. James' money, too, she looked on, if not quite as a personal possession, at least only as his in trust for her little Edward. After all, it could not be of much use to a blind man. Naturally, someone with his affliction could never marry. She had, in fact, persuaded herself that it was very lucky for James that she possessed an Edward for whom all his worldly goods could be saved.

"For good!" he repeated.

"But that's out of the question."

James' voice was exasperated.

"Don't talk rot, Vera. Don was my best friend and the girl's my ward. Where else do you think she's going to go?"

Vera had to hold herself in not to lose her temper.

"Where did you find the chaperone?"

"Through Doctor Ewart."

"Is she old?"

For answer James got up and pressed the bell. "You shall see for yourself."

Marda and Shirley were still gossiping when Tims knocked on the door.

"Mr. Longford says would you go down to the sitting-room to meet Mrs. Cross, Miss?"

Marda waited for the door to shut on Tims, then turned in dismay to Shirley.

"I may be a fool, but do you know I feel nervous."

Shirley threw an arm round her neck.

"Keep up your courage; you'll need it." Then she turned Marda to face her. "We've got to fight this female dog together. You'll see. Friends?"

Marda gave her a kiss. "Friends."

James had a vision of Marda as she would strike Vera. He saw the cluster of yellow curls that Shirley had described, the pink-and-white face, and the big blue eyes. What Vera really saw alarmed her much more. There was one type of person with whom she had never found herself able to cope, and that was the innately honest. She never had a thought which she didn't twist, and a person like Marda, who never had a thought that she did twist, made her feel at a disadvantage. Marda's simplicity and genuineness positively shone out from her.

"Marda, my dear," said James, "this is my sister, Mrs. Cross. Vera, this is Miss Mayne."

Vera gave a kind little nod and held out her hand.

"How do you do, Miss Mayne? You look very young for, the post of chaperone."

Marda's heart had fallen like a stone at the sight of Mrs. Cross; at the same time she had an awful feeling that she was going to smile, because she could not help remembering the description of the cow suffering from flatulence.

"Well, not a chaperone exactly, more a companion."

Vera nodded.

"We must go into that tomorrow. I must run through your duties with you and see how you are managing." She turned to James. "Do you still have your meals alone, or does Shirley have them with you?"

"I have them alone. I have given Shirley the two rooms on the ground floor. She has had them done up."

"Done up!" Vera gasped. "Oh, that was a very naughty brother. You know how little fun I have, and how much I would have enjoyed choosing things."

Marda saw that James was tired and nervous. He answered with an edge on his voice.

"My dear girl, Shirley has to live in the rooms, not you."

Vera felt she had borne enough for the moment. She got up.

"I shall go to my room now and have a weeny rest. You know how journeys tire me, but I always sleep so well in this house, it's so nice and quiet at the back."

Marda scrubbed nervously at the carpet with her toe. "I'm terribly afraid you're not in the back room. The spare room is now the one on the top floor at the front." Vera fixed a steely eye on Marda.

"And who is in my room?"

"Not your room," James interposed, wearily. "It was only a spare bedroom."

Vera's eye never flickered off Marda.

"And who has it now?"

"I do. You see, Shirley has the one in the front and I have the one at the back. They've just been done up."

Vera felt a flush mounting her cheeks. She said to her acquaintances, "I am so fortunate, I can always control my temper." If she could have seen her face when she was controlling it, she would have known that it said everything that she was thinking, and therefore the effort at control was scarcely worthwhile. She succeeded, however, in walking calmly to the door. There she turned.

"Well, goodnight, Miss Mayne. I don't suppose we shall meet again this evening. You, I suppose, have dinner on a tray in your room?"

James tapped his cigarette angrily on the ashtray at his side.

"Of course she doesn't. She has her meals with Shirley. Tonight you will all three dine together. We'll have coffee up here afterwards."

Vera gave a faint sigh.

"Oh, well, I suppose I shall get used to everything."

James looked at Marda as the door shut.

"You mustn't mind. She's an awfully good sort really. She's always looked after me."

Marda laughed.

"Of course I don't mind. And I'll have a tray in my room if she'd rather."

He smiled.

"Don't you get difficult."

If Marda had not been worried as to what effect Mrs. Cross might have on their plans for forcing James to see Mannheim, she would have found the evening funny. Both Vera and Shirley were determined to be the hostess. To ensure this, Vera, in a rather shabby black evening skirt and an unfortunate jumper in green brocade, came down to dinner early and settled herself firmly in Shirley's chair at the head of the table. When the two girls came in, she turned to Shirley with a kind smile.

"There you are, my dear." She looked at Shirley's white evening dress. "You shouldn't bother to put on that frock for me. I've always made a rule in this house there shall be no dressing up. It seems a little unkind, I think, when James can't see."

Shirley sat down with a glint in her eye.

"Well, I guess it's a point of view if you dress only to please the men, but I dress to please myself. I wouldn't feel comfortable looking an old rag-and-bone."

Vera straightened the green jumper.

"Well, of course, perhaps you're a lucky little person with a lot of money to spend on pretty things, but we widows who have to count every penny, and do without lots of nice things because we have an expensive little boy at home, have to content ourselves with very plain frocks. But I don't think we look like rags and bones."

Shirley gulped as though she was going to be sick, so Marda broke in hurriedly:

"How is your little boy?"

Vera turned to her with the hurt expression of one who has been unexpectedly spoken to by a stranger in a bus.

"Yes, Miss Mayne?"

Shirley was not standing for that.

"You can break down and act natural and call her Marda."

Vera unfolded her napkin.

"Perhaps later on, when I know her better." She gave Marda a kind smile. "Such a mistake, I always think, getting on too familiar terms with . . ." She hesitated. "You won't mind if I say employees, will you, dear? I always think the formal relationship is best."

Tims came in with the soup. Shirley and Marda had discussed the dinner over breakfast.

"Let's make old Barlow spread herself," Shirley had said. "What about us having bortsch with a lot of sour cream? And then something done with lobster, and then some game, and then a soufflé."

Marda had been gloomy.

"It's all very well for you, but I've got to go and see Mrs. Barlow."

"I think it'll be worth it," Shirley had explained. "I've a theory it's as well to begin as you mean to go on."

"If you mean to go on like that," Marda had protested, "Mrs. Barlow really will give notice."

Shirley had nodded.

"That's O.K. by me. Let's get right down to it and order the decorations. That louse can't creep out quick enough to please me."

Now with the arrival of the bortsch, Shirley turned graciously to Vera.

"I do hope you like bortsch; I ordered it especially for you."

Vera had been going to give herself a large helping, but at this piece of what she considered rank impertinence, she reduced the ladleful by half.

"I'm surprised Mrs. Barlow agreed. She knows that I like things very plain. I must have a good talk with her tomorrow."

Shirley helped herself to the soup.

"I expect you and Mrs. Barlow get on very well, don't you? Write to each other for Christmas, and all that sort of thing."

Vera had the grace to flush.

"What a funny little person you are! But I always remember to send all the staff a card at Christmas, don't I, Tims?"

Tims took the soup round to Marda. In the kitchen the fact that Mrs. Barlow had written to Mrs. Cross was not exactly an open secret, but it was a whispered one, handed to Mason by Daisy, and from Mason to Tims, and by all three of them to the charlady. He wondered, as he told Mason afterwards, that Mrs. Cross could sit there and face Miss Shirley out, but all he said was:

"Yes, indeed, thank you, Madam."

Regretfully, Vera took a very small portion of cream.

"I must have a look at the household bills; they must be going up by leaps and bounds with all this rich fare."

Shirley ladled cream into her soup.

"I shouldn't bother. You can leave all that to Marda, and Jimmie never minds what he spends."

Vera nearly choked over her soup, mentally seeing little Edward's fortune diminishing with every gulp.

"There are others one must think of besides oneself," she observed, enigmatically.

This seemed to fire Shirley, and as course succeeded course, she burbled on about one extravagance after another. Daimlers hired for country drives. James' presents of frocks. The grand piano, the wirelesses, and the carte blanche she had had in decorating the rooms.

"My!" she said, as the souffle arrived. "He just can't spend money fast enough or quick enough, that man." Vera's gloom was like a dense fog on a November day. In the ordinary way she doted on a soufflé, but at this speech from Shirley she turned from it with a sick face and whispered:

"No, thank you, Tims."

"Never mind," said Shirley, cheerfully. "You'll be able to fill up on the dessert. I'm just crazy on hothouse fruit. I don't know anything to touch English hothouse grapes." Vera could not stand that.

"English hothouse grapes should, I think, be kept for the sick."

Shirley leant across to Marda.

"If she feels that way, you ought to go out tomorrow and see if you could get any of those beautiful peaches. I don't know where they get them so late in the season."

When the grapes arrived, Shirley took half the bunch and Marda a very few, and Vera had to indignantly sit by and watch them eat. However neatly they are eaten, seeing other people eat grapes is not a particularly beautiful sight, and when you are convinced they should not be eaten at all, the sight becomes repulsive. Vera turned over bitter remarks in her head.

"I was shocked when I arrived today to see poor Jim. I think he looks wretched."

Shirley laid down a grape pip.

"Now isn't that strange? His own doctor, who hadn't seen him for months, said he had never seen such an improvement in a man. That's right, isn't it, Marda?"

Marda seized her opportunity.

"He is better, Mrs. Cross. And not only in his health. There's just one chance in a million that something could be done for his sight."

Vera grew rigid. She felt as though she had swallowed a block of ice. It could not be true. Poor dear James was blind. He was going to be blind for the rest of his life and, that being so, there was only one interest in life for him, and that was little Edward. She would have been shocked at herself if she could have heard the inflexion in her voice.

"Who says so?"

Shirley laid down her grapes and quite frankly stared at her. Marda gaped; she had expected, however idiotic this woman was, that this piece of news at least must please her. But her tone of voice! It was astounding.

"Doctor Ewart."

Vera grew slowly red right up her face into her hair. Her words tumbled over each other.

"Then he'd no right to. My brother is blind, and nothing can be done for his eyes. Absolutely nothing, I tell you. It's only raising false hopes in him to talk rubbish like that. Nobody's to mention this subject to him, you understand."

Marda's face was horrified.

"But he has been told. Doctor Ewart wants him to see a man called Mannheim, a Swiss who will be over here next month. We wanted you to help us persuade him."

"Persuade him!" Vera said triumphantly. "Then he won't agree. And perfectly right, too. I shouldn't dream of persuading him. And I absolutely forbid you, Miss Mayne, to mention the subject to him again. In fact, I think it was a gross impertinence of you to talk to me in that way about it. 'We want you to help us' indeed! If I think it right that my poor unfortunate brother should be put to further suffering, I will see to it myself, without any help from you."

Marda could not believe she was hearing aright. She leant across the table.

"Somehow or other I must have put all this very badly. I saw, or thought I saw, that a sudden strong light made Mr. Longford blink. If it's true that the nerves of his eyes are dead, then he couldn't be affected by a sudden strong light, or by anything else. So I went to Doctor Ewart and asked him if he would come and pay a friendly visit and see if I was right. He did. We pulled the curtains together without Mr. Longford knowing why we were doing it, and he tested him with a torch, and it was quite true; definitely Mr. Longford saw something. Doctor Ewart says it's a very slender chance, but if there is one chance in the world he must take it. Surely you agree?"

Vera found what she had been afraid of finding when she first saw Marda. A straightforwardness that acted like a wall. There was no way for her twistings of mind to climb over it or under it. She was conscious, too, that she had shocked both girls. She did not admit that they had any reason to be shocked; her only motive in saying what she had was to keep Jim from any further pain; but girls were silly and sentimental. She reverted to her pose of pathetic little widow.

"Oh, I see. I hadn't understood. As a matter of fact, the idea is so strange, it's so exciting, that it absolutely carried me away. Of course, if there really is a chance, then it's simply too wonderful. Mannheim, you say the name is?" Shirley had taken a cigarette and was lighting it. She looked at it. "If you girls are going to smoke, I think I'll go straight up to Jim. We've always been rather more to each other than just sister and brother, and we do like a teeny time alone together." She turned to Marda. "Thank you for telling me all this, Miss Mayne. And now I want you girls to be very, very sensible and leave it to me to talk to my brother. I know how sensitive he is, and if he is to be persuaded to have himself looked at, then the best thing is to leave the whole thing entirely in my hands."

Marda and Shirley sat staring at each other when the door had shut. Shirley blew a smoke-ring up to the ceiling.

"I wonder if she's got enough power over him to keep him from seeing Mannheim?"

"But she wouldn't," said Marda—"she couldn't. Not now she understands."

Shirley leant across the table.

"Look here, you're dumb, but you can't be that dumb. That woman is downright bad. I guess she doesn't mean to be bad, but that's how she's turned out. She'll soft-soap it all right; she'll say she didn't want Jimmie to have his eyes touched because another operation might kill him, or some such muck; but the plain truth is, it suits her he should be blind."

"But why?"

"Because of the boy, I should guess. He seems to be the only child in the family. Some day she'll expect a big allowance for that kid. What do you suppose all that hooey meant about the house bills? I reckon she's been counting every penny for little Edward."

"But he can still have it."

"Not if he spends it. And, oh boy, would he spend if he could see! Now, look here, Marda, you're rising ten years older than me in years but you're ten years younger than me in sense. You've got to find time tonight or tomorrow and get right down to this Mannheim business. If you don't, old snake-in-the-grass Cross will have us scotched."

"But why me?" said Marda. "Why not you?"

Shirley sighed and stubbed out her cigarette.

"There are days when I feel it would be fun to get around with somebody who'd stopped wearing crawlers."

CHAPTER ELEVEN

VERA was a woman of tenacity of purpose. Having made up her mind to a thing, she went to great pains to see it through. Although she had a mass of shopping to do, and a dentist to visit, she sacrificed these minor needs to the greater need of keeping a vigilant eye on James.

An inspection of the house on the morning after she arrived showed a state of affairs that she found very disturbing. The servants, always before people she had described as 'models,' had, to her way of thinking, been 'got at.' It started with Mason when she brought in her morning tea.

"Good morning," said Vera, sitting up in bed.

"I hope you slept well, Madam," Mason replied.

Vera let out what was meant to be a pathetic little fluttering sigh, but was actually a good hearty breath.

"Not very, I'm afraid. When you've had rather a sad, hard life, sleeping is difficult." She poured out her tea. "And I must admit I was a weeny bit disappointed not to have my usual bed. That mattress, that I had learned to call my own, seemed to rock me to sleep. This one is not as comfy."

Mason was drawing back the curtains; she turned now, on the defensive.

"But you have got your own mattress, Madam. I carried it up myself with the help of Mrs. Jones, the charlady. 'Take the mattress off my bed, Mason,' Miss Mayne said; 'I expect Mrs. Cross is used to that one.'"

Vera was set back, but she was not going to show it.

"Really! How funny. It felt quite different. Then it must have been the room; it is much noisier in the front than at the back."

Mason flicked open the last of the curtains.

"Not last night it wasn't. There was a drunk and a girl having a proper set-to. She screamed at him, and he bawled at her. There was none of us that sleep at the back got a wink while it was going on."

Vera felt as if she had walked down a cul-de-sac. She eyed Mason disapprovingly; she did not care for her tone, and from Mason a tone that she did not care for was a shock. She changed her tactics.

"It must make a lot of work for you having the two young ladies in the house."

Mason gave a quick eye round to see that the room was in order.

"None that I can't manage, Madam." She went quietly and respectfully out of the room.

Vera looked at the shut door resentfully.

"It only shows," she told herself, "how quickly a bad influence affects the whole house."

Vera tackled Tims after breakfast. He was standing over Mrs. Jones and tapping a great vase of chrysanthemums.

"Miss Mayne changes the water herself and there's no need for you to touch them. They take her a terrible time to arrange, so you be careful."

Mrs. Jones looked at the chrysanthemums admiringly.

"Lovely, ain't they! Put you in mind of a flower show."

Tims nodded.

"That's right. So you be careful of your duster."

Vera came into the hall just as Tims said these last words. She had studied Shirley's sitting-room and been appalled at the expensive flowers massed everywhere. The sight of Tims and Mrs. Jones apparently gloomily regarding yet another extravagant collection brought her over to them.

"These flowers make a lot of work, I'm afraid, Tims."

Tims turned at the sound of her voice.

"Oh no, Madam. Miss Mayne sees to them. She gets them twice a week from Covent Garden."

Mrs. Jones felt she was being left out of the conversation.

"It's not so bad in the chrysanth season; it's the summer things get you down. All those blue flowers dropping on the carpet."

Vera made clicking sympathetic sounds.

"Don't I know! And really it's quite unnecessary. My poor brother never cared for flowers even when he could see them."

Tims in the ordinary way would have let that pass, but Mason had been at him.

"If 'She' tries to get you to run the young ladies down, don't you stand for it. You answer up bold, same as I did."

Since the great expedition to the dogs Mason and Tims had been out together once or twice. Sometimes to a picture and now and again to a music hall. Tims enjoyed these expeditions, but he occasionally suspected that Mason considered he was rather lacking in spirit. He knew that all women liked a brave, forward man, and he was trying to seem rather more that type. This was plainly an opportunity.

"He has changed, then, Madam. Takes a great interest in the flowers now. Why, only yesterday, when he and Miss Mayne were going out, he stopped just where you are standing now and he said, 'What's that smell?' And she told him to go and sniff at them and guess, and he did and he said, 'Are they the golden-brown kind?' And when she said they were he was ever so pleased."

Vera disliked this story intensely.

"All the same," she said, "the flowers must be cut down. It's ridiculous spending all that money when there are so many needy persons about."

Tims and Mrs. Jones watched Vera go up the stairs. Then Mrs. Jones winked.

"I'd take a bet who the needy ones are, Mr. Tims."

Tims was too good a servant to allow that.

"Then you must keep your ideas to yourself, Mrs. Jones."

It was with a cosy feeling of being two people with a single mind that Vera and Mrs. Barlow settled down for a talk. It was ecstasy to Mrs. Barlow to pour out her woes.

"It's not that I can't cook the things, though all the help I have is that Daisy who's worse than useless, but it's not reasonable. I cooked for the late Mr. and Mrs. Longford, and I think I know what ladies and gentlemen need. But all this new-fangled stuff, Russian this and French that, it's enough to drive you crazy."

"And the books, I suppose, terrible?"

Mrs. Barlow raised her eyebrows.

"Shocking. You wouldn't believe what we spend."

Vera could, and did, believe any figure however enormous, and shuddered.

"I am going to put a stop to that, of course."

Mrs. Barlow was standing by, and Vera sitting at, the kitchen table. Now Mrs. Barlow leant down and reduced her voice to a whisper.

"You can't put a stop to anything while they're here. This is no house for Miss Shirley; she's running wild. And if she went, Miss Mayne would go; and if you ask me, that's where the trouble lies. She's a sly one, that. Looks as if butter wouldn't melt in her mouth and always so full of Mr. Longford likes this, and Mr. Longford likes that; but I've eyes in my head. I can see what's going on. Mr. Longford may be blind, poor gentleman, but he's rich, and when you come of a family that hasn't threepence to rub together, it's the money that counts."

Vera felt cold. Could this be true? Could this Mayne girl be trying to marry James? It was unthinkable. If money was spent like this now, how would it be when she had control of it? If she had control of it, what would happen to little Edward? Where would the big allowance come from to educate him, give him a good time at Oxford, and start him off on a career?

"What have you heard or seen that makes you think this?"

Mrs. Barlow pursed up her lips.

"I don't need to hear and see. I have my intuition, and my intuition takes me a lot further than most people's eyes and ears. Besides, what about commonsense? What would you feel if you were nearer thirty than twenty, and plain? Wouldn't you wheedle your way in where you saw the chance, and cheat someone into believing they couldn't live without you?"

"You think she's doing that?"

Mrs. Barlow shrugged her shoulders.

"Trying to; but I wouldn't say she had got there. But it was high time you came along, 'm, to show her what's what."

"But it's Miss Shirley he seems fond of, if either of them."

"Oh, her!" Mrs. Barlow dismissed Shirley with a sniff. "She's one as has to have all the men lie down and make a carpet for her to walk on, and once they're down she'll wipe her feet on them. She can do it too, with her looks."

Vera got up.

"I don't consider her particularly good looking; I don't admire the type. In any case, her looks can't affect my poor brother, because he can't see."

"A couple of cats can't see each other in the dark, but they get up on the roof just the same. But it's not Miss Shirley is the trouble, 'm. You do as I say and get Miss Shirley away, and what is troublesome'll have to go too."

Fired by this conversation, Vera scuttled up the stairs to James' room. Talking to Mrs. Barlow, she had left him alone too long; there was no knowing what that hussy might be up to.

Marda was reading to James. They were through the political news and were in the middle of an article on boxing when Vera opened the door. James, looking happy and interested, was lolling back in his chair; his pipe in his mouth. The windows were open and the sun streaming in, but because it was cold there was a log fire. On the table by James, and on the mantelpiece, were bowls of roses. Marda had pulled a humpty up to the fireside; she was so at ease now in this room, and so contented to be with James, that she looked permanent and as if she belonged. Vera took in the whole atmosphere in one snorting breath. Her voice came out cracked and harsh.

"What are you doing in here, Miss Mayne?"

Marda had stopped reading as the door opened. She looked at Vera in surprise.

"Reading to Mr. Longford. I do every morning."

Vera hurried across the room and almost snatched the paper from her.

"Well, you needn't when I am in the house."

Marda got up uncertainly.

"Oh, very well—I'm sorry."

James, irritated at the interruption, turned his head to Vera. "What is it, my dear?"

Vera returned with a bump to her pathetic widowed-sister voice. She came to him and kissed him.

"Nothing, little brother. Only I wanted to read to you, so I was telling Miss Mayne she could go." With the hand that was not on James' shoulder she made a gesture to Marda to get out of the room. "Now, what shall I read? But first you must hear a letter Eddie has written to his Mum-mum."

James was no fonder of hearing children's letters read out loud than any other uncle. He was cross and looked it.

"But Miss Mayne reads to me every day." The door shut behind Marda. "There, she's gone. Blast it all, Vera, why do you want to read to me? You never have before."

Vera gave some little pats to his shoulder which she intended to be soothing, but which were actually maddening.

"Who's a crossums! I know sisters shouldn't interfere, but I think that Miss Mayne is a young person better kept in her place."

James pulled away from her.

"Do stop pawing me, my dear. Marda's all right; you needn't worry about her."

Vera pulled a chair over beside him. She had a theory that the closer you sat to blind people, the more likely they were to hear. She forced a friendly, worldly-wise voice.

"Look here, old man, you don't know it, being a bachelor, but you can't go on running the house like this. Shirley is running wild and Miss Mayne has absolutely no control over her."

James bit on his pipe.

"It seems to be working all right."

"But it isn't. We women know things that sometimes miss you men, and I can feel there is something wrong in this house. I felt it the moment I came in at the front door. Something not very nice, Jim dear."

James tapped out his pipe on his ashtray and got up. His tone closed the discussion.

"You let your imagination run away with you. I hear it's a lovely morning. I think I shall go out for a bit."

"Out! My dear Jim, I thought you hated the idea of being seen in the streets."

He felt his way to the door.

"I go straight across to the Park. We never meet anybody, and Marda tells me nobody stares."

Vera followed him to the door.

"That girl would tell you anything. Anyway, my dear boy, if you feel like a walk this morning, it's splendid, and I will go with you."

Vera was in a bad temper. Her horror of seeing the only money there was for her boy passing into other hands made her behave in a way of which she would have been ashamed if she had stopped to analyse her motives, or had the ability to analyse them. If she had heard a description of what she did that morning about another person she would have been horrified. As she and James walked to the Park, she kept up a running commentary on those people they passed and on what she saw.

"It makes one feel quite conspicuous walking with you. Not nastily, of course; people only look sympathetic and in the kindest way."

"There, there's a little boy—be careful, little boy, this is a poor blind man, you wouldn't want to hit him with your dirty hoop, would you?"

"It's wonderful how an affliction in other people brings out the best in everybody, isn't it? That was quite a shabby poor man we passed, and he moved right to one side to let you go by."

It was a lovely morning, but in no time James had turned.

"Let's go back, old girl. I'd like a taxi."

After lunch, Vera took her sewing into James' room. He was sitting listlessly, doing nothing. The morning had depressed him so utterly he had not troubled to put on the wireless. Vera held out the arm of a small shirt.

"I wish you could see what I am doing. A little blue Viyella shirt for Eddie. Such a pretty colour and it exactly matches his eyes. Won't he look a duck?" She did not wait for James to answer, but burbled on. "Tell me, dear boy, Shirley and Miss Mayne said something to me last night about you wanting to see a man about your eyes. What exactly are you planning?"

James had had more than enough of his eyes for one day. With horror it was dawning on him that he had let himself fell into the very weakness which he had fought for six years to avoid. He had fought against being a burden and being petted, and now he had allowed two girls to make a fool of him, to pretend that he was nearly a normal man and that they liked being seen about with him. He pictured how they had been looking in the Park. He on little golden-haired Marda's arm, like some horrible illustration given away in a Christmas supplement in the Victorian era. Marda had never said, nor had Shirley, that people were staring and nudging, but now he knew it was true. Vera, who wouldn't trouble to be tactful, had let the cat out of the bag.

"It's a pack of nonsense," he snapped. "I'm having nothing done to my eyes and I don't want the matter discussed."

Vera stitched at the small cuff in her hand.

"I think you are right. I own I would have been a very frightened sister. You went through such tortures last time, I couldn't bear the thought of you having all that to suffer again, and almost certainly for nothing."

James had his mind still fixed on the way Marda and Shirley had fooled him; he did not bother to focus on what Vera was saying.

"If I were to send Shirley to live somewhere else, where could she go? Not to you in Devon; she's had a dull enough time here, poor child! Now I want to make it up to her by giving her a good time."

Vera felt as if she had been battling through a wood full of scrub which caught at her feet, and had come out to a smooth field and easy walking. She was prepared for any idea for Shirley so long as she got her out of the way. It might come expensive, but it was a limited expense and worth while if it cleared the two girls out of the house.

"How about sending her to someone for a season? I believe very nice women, peeresses and so on, offer to chaperone girls for a consideration."

James made a face.

"I always picture them as frightful old hags. All the same, Shirley might find it fun." He looked towards Vera gratefully. "That's not at all a bad idea. I'll put it up to the child this evening."

Vera's face was smug.

"If she likes the idea I'll start enquiries at once. I believe you always do that sort of thing through an agency. I expect you would like to get the two girls away as quickly as possible. Miss Mayne will, of course, go home."

James was fidgeting with his hands, his expression hidden. His voice was lifeless.

"Yes, she'll go home."

Vera and James were still sitting talking when Shirley bounced in from the art school. She flung her arms round James and sat on the arm of his chair.

"Hullo, Jimmie, how's things?" She took his face in her two hands and turned it towards her. "My! What have you been doing to yourself? You look terrible."

James jerked his head away, irritably.

"I'm perfectly all right."

Shirley got up slowly and moved away, keeping an eye on Vera.

"What have you two been talking about?"

Vera laid down her sewing.

"Inquisitive little person! As a matter of fact we've been talking about you. We were thinking it would be a good idea for you to go and stay with a society chaperone for a season."

"Oh, yeh? You mean Marda and I will clear out of this house?"

Vera nodded.

"Yes, dear."

"And you and little Edward move right in?" Vera relapsed definitely into a pathetic little widow.

"Oh, I'm afraid not. Eddie and his Mummum have to live in the country; it's so terribly 'spensive in London."

Shirley did not answer for a moment; she just looked at Vera, then she went to the door. Halfway there she paused.

"I was always told that if you live in a snake country you need to keep an eye out all the time, for the things keep moving through the grass so sneaky you can't hear them, and the first thing you know you get a bite and a load of poison. I guess that's right, don't you?"

Vera looked at her doubtfully.

"I've no idea what you are talking about."

"No?" Shirley took hold of the door handle. "Well, maybe I'll write it out for you; you can read it over when you're in bed."

Marda was in her room. Shirley bounced in without knocking and flung herself on the bed.

"She's done us. She's got at Jimmie. Unless we work pretty snappily we're out."

Marda's eyes were wide and dark with fright, and all the colour drained from her cheeks.

"Out!"

Shirley repeated the conversation that she had had with Vera.

"And the worst of it is, it's a darned good idea. You can't say it's mean, you can't say it isn't what I'd like. It's just one of those things you can't take hold of."

"Would you like it?"

Shirley shook her head.

"I'm not leaving this house yet awhile, nor are you." She leant against the bed head. "Poor Jimmie, he's looking just awful. Kind of low and crushed. Like he used to be when I first came."

Marda came over to her.

"Do you think she's spoken to him about his eyes?"

"I wouldn't wonder. That means you've got to say your say today."

Marda made a despairing gesture.

"How can I? I haven't seen him all day. I read the paper to him for a little while this morning, but she took it from me and turned me out of the room. You know how sensitive he is. It isn't the kind of thing you can just blurt into just any old way. I've got to have the time and he's got to be in the mood."

"Mood!" Shirley sat up. "Tonight's the night. We'll have liqueurs with our coffee. Maybe she's not used to them and will get drowsy and go early to bed. Then I'll leave you to have your word."

Marda was doubtful.

"If he's in a bad mood already, today's a rotten day."

Shirley shrugged her shoulders.

"Maybe. But if you let that snake-in-the-grass get at him for a week we're as good as finished. You get a promise out of him to see Mannheim and he'll stick to it. Jimmie's not the sort to break his word."

Marda looked at her watch.

"It's teatime. Better be going down." She went to the dressing-table and ran a comb disconsolately through her hair. "Oh, goodness, I wish she hadn't come."

Shirley laid down her liqueur glass.

"My! Those drinks have warmed me up. I think I'll go and play the piano. Can you stand a little music, Jimmie?" She didn't wait for him to answer, fearing a refusal, but ran out of the room and down the stairs.

"I don't know what Shirley gave me in that glass," said Vera, "but I feel quite confused." She turned kindly to Marda. "Don't you think this is a splendid scheme for Shirley? It's so wretchedly dull for her in this house."

Marda looked her in the eye.

"She's been happy here."

Vera smiled.

"And of course it's been a very nice job for you. But we must think of other people sometimes, mustn't we? I'm sure you needn't worry; my brother will give you a good reference and you can soon get something else."

Shirley had struck a few chords on the piano, the music came rolling up the stairs. "Carry me back to old Virginia."

"Dear me, that girl has got quite a good voice, almost like a professional."

"She does everything well," said Marda.

James turned his head at the sound of her voice.

"Marda"—he hesitated, speaking in the nervous way he had when she first came to the house—"this won't make any difference to you—I mean, you had a contract with me and it will go on until you get something else. You do understand?"

Vera was slightly bemused by liqueurs.

"I think he must leave that sort of thing to me, don't you, Miss Mayne? Men are so silly and quixotic about money."

Marda felt sick. This discussion of her salary, as if money entered into the question at all! That James should think that she would mind leaving the house because she would be out of work! She got up.

"I'm—I'm tired. I think I will go to bed if nobody minds. Goodnight."

Vera waited until Marda was out of hearing.

"Selfish, you know. Gone off in a huff because of our little scheme for Shirley. Quite ridiculous, for I'm sure she can get something else if she tries."

Shirley had stopped singing, now she started again.

"There is a lady sweet and kind,

Was never face so pleas'd my mind;"

"Dear old song," said Vera; "it's always been a favourite with me." She joined in the singing in a shrill, throaty voice.

James crashed his fist on the table beside her.

"Shut up! Shut up!" Vera stared at him, her mouth open as she clung to the word "die." James pulled himself together. "I'm sorry. I'm tired or something. Tell that child to stop playing."

Vera, quite scared, bustled out of the door.

"Her gestures, motions, and her smile,

Her wit, her voice my heart beguile—

Beguile my heart I know not why,
And yet I love her.

Vera had reached Shirley—the song broke off abruptly.

Because James was obviously overstrained, Vera made it an excuse and bustled Shirley up to bed. She was glad that there was an excuse handy, for, thanks to the liqueurs, she was dropping with sleep.

Shirley gave an appearance of going to bed, but actually she only waited until Vera's door was shut and then she slipped along to Marda's room and knocked.

"Who's that?" Marda called.

"Shirley."

Marda's voice was muffled.

"Do you mind, darling, if you don't come in? I'm awfully tired."

Shirley wriggled with impatience.

"Let me in, you idiot. I've got to speak to you." Marda unlocked the door and then, before Shirley was in, had hurried to her wardrobe, where she seemed very busy.

Shirley, quite unmoved by this manoeuvre, followed her and gripped her arm and turned her round.

"All right. I know you've been crying. No need to hide it. I don't think that cow's worth crying over, but if you do that's your business."

Marda's eyes were red and swollen.

"It wasn't her, exactly. It was her and Mr. Longford thinking I didn't want to leave just because of the money, and really it's because I'm fond of you, and—"

Shirley pulled her out of the cupboard.

"I know, it's only because of me you mind going. It's a beautiful world, isn't it? Now let's drop telling each other fairytales and get down to sense. You're to go right down to Jimmie now. He's needing you."

"Needing me?"

"Yes. He's all to pieces. You go and soothe him down, and while you're at it push the Mannheim talk home. I doubt if he'll listen, but you've got to try."

"But I can't. I'm undressed."

Shirley, for answer, opened the door.

"A blind man can't see a dressing-gown, and if he could I guess he'd stand up to it. Go on, scram. And go down quietly; you don't want old snake-in-the-grass hearing you."

James was so deep in his own misery that he did not hear Marda as she opened his door. He was leaning forward, his head slumped into his hands. He had not realised until today how happy he had grown. He had become so dried up in the six years of his blindness that only by minute degrees could happiness ooze its way into him, and when at last he was soaked through with it, he had taken it for granted, and accepted that he was newborn.

Now in one day Vera had crushed him and wrung the happiness out of him. He had been living in a fool's paradise. He had been right when he knew there was no world for him among ordinary men and women.

Marda forgot herself, looking at James. Pity welled up in her and took possession of her. He was hurt—it showed in every line of him. She must comfort him. She was across the room in one second and her arms were round him.

"Oh, my dear, what is it? Can't I help?"

James raised his head. He spoke in a whisper.

"Marda!"

"Darling," she said, holding him closer. "Oh, darling."

Suddenly he stiffened, sat straighter and took hold of her arms and held them from him.

"No. I don't want that. I don't want pity."

Marda was too full of her feeling for him to care what he said to her. She forced her arms back.

"Pity! I haven't any right to be sitting here with my arms round you, but it's not pity that makes me do it. It's because I'm fond of you."

He turned his head as if to be sure he had heard properly.

"Fond! Marda, you can't be."

She misunderstood his inflexion.

"Yes, I am, but it doesn't matter. I mean I'm quite happy to go on being fond and not expecting any fondness back. I . . ."

He had her in his arms.

"Marda, you're not really fond of me? Don't fool me. You see, I love you."

He was holding her so tightly that she had to wriggle to get her mouth free to answer.

"I've loved you from the first day I met you."

"It can't be true. Oh, my dear, but why? I haven't dared to hope. Just once I did, but then you snubbed me and drew back, and I understood. Why should you care for a blind man?"

"As if blindness had anything to do with it. You love people because you can't help it. What they are like, if they are deaf or blind, or got an arm or leg missing, doesn't mean anything at all."

"Then why did you snub me? There was that night when you held my hand. I didn't know I could be so happy."

"Nor did I. You said 'the time of the singing of birds is come.'"

She was kneeling at his feet; now he had one arm round her and the other hand was exploring her face, feeling her hair, her eyes, and the curve of her mouth.

"I thought it had that night. Then the next day you changed. Why did you, Marda?"

She did not answer for a moment, uncertain what would be loyal to say.

"I thought you cared for Shirley, and she for you."

He kissed her before he answered.

"Little fool. Shirley's a darling, but I'd as soon love a Pekinese."

"Perhaps she cares for you."

"Not she. She's a minx; she has to have every man on his knees, whether it's your small brother or a crock like myself, but once we're there she loses interest."

"I'm not sure." Marda held the hand that was stroking her hair. "Please don't tell her about us. I'd hate her to be hurt."

He smiled.

"You tell her. You'll see I'm right. Shirley has no real use for me, even if I weren't blind."

That reminded Marda of her reason for being there. "James."

He kissed her again.

"Not that. Jim's better."

"Well, Jim, then. Please I want you to do something for me."

"Anything you say. You know that."

"Will you please see Mannheim?" She felt him contract. "I know you hate the idea, but please see him."

"He can't do anything for me."

"Dr. Ewart thinks he might."

"It's such a hell of a lot of messing about for nothing." Marda knelt upright and held his face in her hands.

"I don't ask this for me. I love you just the same, whether you're blind or not. But if you love me, you'll do this to please me."

James was silent for a moment. Then he hugged her to him, kissing her and speaking through his kisses.

"I love you. I love you. I'll see anybody you like if it makes you happy."

Unheard, the door opened, and Vera's face peered in. Vera was a proper woman, and her eyes bulged and her cheeks flamed at what she saw.

"Miss Mayne!"

Blushing, Marda tried to pull away from James, but he held her tighter and grinned over her head at Vera.

"Hullo, my dear. You've come in at exactly the right moment. Miss Mayne has promised to marry me."

Vera swallowed several times. She was confused by the news and still confused by liqueurs.

"I don't believe it. Even you couldn't be such a fool."

"My dear Vera . . ." he protested. But she wouldn't let him finish. Instead she turned to Marda, stammering in anger.

"As for you, Miss Mayne, have you taken leave of your senses? Have you thought of the future, tied for the rest of your life to a man who has to be led everywhere, who—"

Marda pulled away from James and faced Vera.

"If I have to lead him all the rest of my life, I'll be glad to do it. But I don't believe for a moment I'll have to. He's going to see Mannheim, and I believe he can save his eyes."

Vera, seeing her hopes for Edward receding further and further, entirely lost her head.

"Rubbish! I won't hear of it. It's torturing you for nothing, Jim. The man is probably a quack and will insist on operating in order to get the fee, and then you'll die on the operating-table and then where will you be?"

James chuckled.

"I shouldn't like to say, my dear. Up or down." He groped for and found Marda's hand.

"It's all right, darling. You have my promise. I won't be scared off."

Vera's voice broke on a note of hysteria.

"You trapped him into this, sneaking about in your night things. Behaving I don't know how. How you dare carry on in this way with that defenceless child upstairs, I don't know."

At the thought of Shirley described as a defenceless child, both Marda and James began to laugh. James came over to Vera and put his aim round her shoulders.

"Don't be a fool, my dear. I can't see Marda's clothes. I'd no idea she had her nightdress on. And I really wouldn't worry about Shirley. You go up to bed. Take her up, Marda."

He held out his hand to her as he spoke, and Marda came over and kissed him goodnight.

"Bless you!" he whispered. "Bless you!"

Vera refused all assistance from Marda and strode up the stairs to her bedroom without a goodnight and with a back rigid with resentment.

Marda paused outside Shirley's bedroom. Would she be asleep? Should she tell her? She decided against it. It was going to be a ticklish business telling Shirley, and just for this one night she wanted her happiness unspoilt. Nothing could take away from that happiness, but tears from Shirley would mar it. As she came into her bedroom, she saw a note on the pillow. She opened it in surprise. It was written in Shirley's large, sprawling handwriting. It said:

"Don't tell me. I've guessed the worst.

SHIRLEY."

CHAPTER TWELVE

MANNHEIM had taken a consulting-room and waiting-room in Harley Street for the duration of his London visit. In spite of the happiness that had come to James since he had become engaged to Marda, it was with cold, blank terror that he faced his interview. Nobody but himself knew what he had gone through in the days following the accident that had lost him his sight; the uneasy sleep which he fought against falling into because he could not face waking up to the horror of finding himself blind; the pain; the nightmare darkness. It had been during those black days in the nursing home that he had made his plan for living out the rest of his life. It was then that he remembered the old house that his aunt and uncle had left; he forgot its vile furniture and its depressed, pale-faced servants, and only knew that there he could creep in, slink into a corner, and lick his wounds unseen.

Practically from the moment that she had come into the house James had known that he loved Marda, though he had fought against the knowledge, shying from sentimental words, for how could Marda love a maimed thing like himself? But love, even if it is fought against, is an expanding influence. There is very little room for phobias in the mind of a person in love, and so it was possible for what amounted to a miracle to take place. By slow stages he had stepped out of his voluntary prison into the world outside, and now, the greatest miracle of all, he had agreed to this interview.

In his first ecstasy at hearing Marcia say she loved him, James had given his promise that he would consult Mannheim, and he had stuck to it, but that in no way mitigated the horror of the visit. To make the affair as little formal as possible, both Marda and Shirley drove to Harley Street with him. It had been Doctor Ewart's idea.

"You two had better come along," he had said to Marda. "He's such a stubborn fellow that I haven't dared to suggest sedatives or anything of that sort, but it's my belief that he hasn't slept for days. If you get to a point when you accept that you are afraid of something and decided to run away from it, you may screw yourself up to doing it, but it's a shocking physical strain, and anything we can do to mitigate it will help him later on. We don't want him going through too much now if an operation is necessary."

Doctor Ewart was waiting for them at Harley Street. He put his arm through James'; his voice was quiet but full of confidence.

"There you are. Mannheim's ready for you." James unconsciously clipped Marda's hand, which was through his other arm closer to his side. Doctor Ewart saw the gesture. "She'll just be in the waiting-room." As he spoke he gave a slight gesture with his head to show the two girls which way to go, and that the time had come for them to leave James. Marda squeezed James' hand.

"Good luck! Don't be scared. Remember nothing's going to happen to you today, and nothing need happen to you ever unless you say so."

Mannheim was a little man with a head reminiscent of St. Peter's. He spoke bad but fluent English.

"Good afternoon, Mr. Longford. This is Doctor Freddie Littlejohn. You cannot see him, but he is good-looking in just the way that we so much admire Englishmen to be." He pushed James gently into a chair and sat down beside him. "Now I am going to ask your good Doctor Ewart and this Doctor Little-john to go away, so that you and I may get to know each other, my friend. It is easier for any test that I shall make that you understand exactly what I am going to do, so that you do not draw yourself together, and resist saying always to yourself, 'That will hurt—this will hurt!'" He waited while the two doctors went out of the room, then he patted James' knee. "I have had a little life story of you from your good Doctor Ewart, and I will, if I may, repeat it, and you will say me if I am wrong."

James, with every nerve in his body taut, tried not to make his voice as resentful as he felt.

"All right, go ahead."

"You were driving in a motor race when you have your acci-dent, and you were thrown out on your head, and you have recovered to find that you are blind. The doctor who treats you at that time has died, and so, although you had been told to come and see him, you accept that you are blind, and you have not been examine since. Now," Mannheim's voice dropped, "this was all six years ago, and so it might have gone on, if it were not for a lady. You're engaged, Mr. Longford, to a Miss

Mayne, who is very intelligent young lady, a dispenser herself, and the daughter of a doctor, and she sees signs that give her to hope, and so she goes to Doctor Ewart."

James stiffened, and Mannheim gave his knee a friendly pat.

"I know you are being so British, and saying to yourself, how dare this nasty little Swiss mention my fiancée's name! I mention it, Mr. Longford, because I am hoping to find a condition which may give cause for hope, and which should give you cause for hope. When a woman loves she doesn't care whether the man has two legs or one, whether he has his eyes or whether he has not; but it would be a so beautiful wedding present if I could hand her to you and say, 'Now he can see.'"

James moved restlessly.

"I know all that, but you can't work a miracle—the nerves of my eyes are dead. I don't know much about the workings of things like eyes, but I know enough to realise that when that happens there's nothing you can do."

"That is so, but I am going to make some experiments in the hope of finding they were not dead. I want you to imagine, Mr. Longford, a river, and from that river there are two little streams, and in those streams the water plants grow. Now, one day there comes a landslide, and somewhere up that river the earth she tumbles in, and the water she ceases to flow. Now, what would happen to those two little streams? They would dry up, and in course of time what grew there would seem to die. But if we should lift the boulders and earth that made the dam to the water, then presently the streams flow again, and you would see, not at first, but little by little, the flowering things come back. Now, that is how it may be with your sight. When you fell, some part of your bone may have been dented or crushed, and it may be pressing on that life-giving water-way which feeds those streams which are your eyes; and it is because of that hope that I am now going to put this room into darkness and make some experiments with light. I am going, in fact, to put a thin trickle of water through the streams, to see if life is still stirring. I will now call Doctor Ewart and Doctor Littlejohn, and perhaps"—he hesitated—"Miss Mayne is with you, is she not? Would you like me to fetch her too, so that she may see exactly what we seek to find, and can talk it over with you afterwards."

James was easier now. It was always hard for him to get used to strangers, and the coming and going of people that he did not know frayed his nerves, but by now he was accustomed to Mannheim, and had got a pretty clear picture of him in his mind. It would be very nice to have Marda in the room. If they were really going to make the room dark, he could hold her hand, and holding it he might forget all the fooling about that they wanted to do.

"Who's this Doctor Littlejohn?" he asked. "What's he in on the business for?"

"He is very clever young man that one. He has been with me in Switzerland, and he was going to work on my lectures over here. But he need not be in the room at the moment if you do not wish. He have been present at many of such tests and has little to learn."

"Well, let's have Marda, then. Littlejohn can look after my ward Shirley. Don't want a gallery of people watching a thing like this."

Marda came in and sat down by James. She took his hand; she said nothing, but gave it a squeeze. Mannheim darkened the room and turned to James with a chuckle.

"Doctor Littlejohn, though he have not said so, is very very grateful that you do not need him. He have but one interest in eyes at the moment, and that is to look at those of the pretty little ward in the next room. Never have I seen Doctor Freddie so discomposed; he look as you say in England, bowl over. Now"—he pressed a button and a thin pencil of light shone on to James' face—"we must get down to our work."

In the other room Freddie Littlejohn was, as Mannheim said, completely bowled over. He had spent a large part of his adolescent days in fancying himself in love with this girl and that girl, but when he set eyes on Shirley, he knew in one blinding flash that this was the real thing.

Shirley was enchanted. She had come with James to Harley Street out of kindness of heart, and because she was really fond of him, and never had she supposed that there could be any pleasure in the afternoon; but the moment that the door had opened and Freddie walked in, she saw that for once in a way a good act was going to be rewarded. She never consciously considered her own reactions towards any man; she just knew the moment that one came within eye-able distance of her, she reacted, and she considered, or would have considered, had it ever happened, that the bottom had fallen out of her world if the man were not in a state of jelly in the space of five minutes. Her only failure in this respect had been James, and that, though she knew why she had been a failure, still rankled with her when she thought of it. It was therefore no surprise to her when she saw Freddie going through all the preliminary stages that led up to infatuation, and it was with gloom that she heard Mannheim's step in the passage.

Shirley was never one to beat about the bush, and so as the door closed on Marda, Mannheim and Doctor Ewart, she smiled.

"Well, say, that makes you believe in fairies, doesn't it?"

Freddie never stammered, but he stammered now.

"I say—well, I mean—you don't mean, do you, that you wanted to talk to me?"

Shirley lowered her eyes, and looked more like a Lenci Madonna than usual.

"Well, I was never crazy on *Punch*. I guess it's being educated in America, but the jokes seem kind of quiet, so I'll be glad of someone to talk to."

Freddie was in the mood to be grateful even to being preferred to back numbers of *Punch*.

"I say, that's awfully nice of you. You know, I suppose you'll think this awful cheek, but I can't help staring at you. You know you're the most beautiful person I've ever met, Miss Kay."

Shirley raised her eyes slowly, so that he could see the full beauty of her lashes.

"That's just darling of you. But nuts on Miss Kay—you can call me Shirley."

Freddie turned crimson.

"Can I? Well, that's awfully nice of you. I say, are you doing anything tonight?"

Part of Shirley's technique was always to be doing something the first two or three times she had an invitation from a new man, and it was a surprise to herself to find her mind running over the night's engagement.

"Well, I am, really. There's a little sort of dance at my art school, but maybe I needn't go."

"Needn't you? I say, then, could you dine and dance with me? We can go anywhere you like."

Shirley beamed. One of the drawbacks to England, from her point of view, was that though she now met plenty of men, or at least boys, they were mostly poor, and were seldom able to say they would go anywhere she liked. She had, too, a new and quite exquisite evening frock that was just asking to be worn.

"Well, now, how about the Savoy? I like the orchestra."

"The Savoy does it," Freddie agreed eagerly. "What time shall I call for you? Will your guardian mind your going out with me?"

Shirley laughed.

"No, I guess I can fix that. Anyway, he's so keyed up just now what with his eyes and getting engaged to Marda that he hardly notices if I'm around. He had a sister who tried to interfere, but she moved off the day after the engagement leaked out." She considered Freddie thoughtfully. "Funny you being a doctor. You don't look like one."

"What do I look like?"

"Well, more like an actor, maybe. You keen on this doctoring?"

Freddie nodded.

"Yes. I've been under Mannheim. He's an absolute wizard. I'm going to specialise on his lines over here."

Shirley was suddenly serious.

"D'you suppose there's really a chance for Jimmie? That's my guardian."

Freddie was at once professional.

"Can't say. I haven't seen him, but there is a condition which Mannheim may discover, and if it's there it means an operation. A very delicate affair, but it would be worth trying."

Shirley lay back in her chair.

"My, I hope something can be done. I'm just crazy about Jimmie; he's just the grandest man. But it isn't only for him. Marda is just the nicest person; if anyone deserves a break she does. Mind you, she doesn't mind marrying him though he's blind, but I'd say it would be kind of hard. There's a lot of fun you'd miss. I reckon that when you marry a man you want to be able to share the things you can see just as much as anything else. You'd want him to be able to see you, and it would make you kind of mad if he couldn't see your babies."

Freddie looked more adoring than ever.

"That's quite right. You've thought a lot for somebody of your age, Shirley."

Shirley turned pink.

"Well, that's funny. I never did get round to thinking that way before. It's just come to me now. Sort of thinking out loud."

"Go on," said Freddie. "Think out loud some more about being married. I like it."

*

The nursing home smelt of ether and hot-house flowers. In the waiting-room where Marda and Shirley sat there was a secretary's desk, and now and again the secretary darted in and checked off lists of gifts for the patients; sheaves of roses, dozens of carnations, huge-headed chrysanthemums all in crackling paper.

"As long as I live I shall remember this room," thought Marda, her breath short and her heart thumping against her ribs. "I'm sure in all my nightmares I'll see these white walls and that mantelpiece and the secretary in her green linen coat with that awful bright expression on her face. I wonder if they have to look bright so as to cheer up the waiting friends and relations, or whether they look bright naturally because when you live forever on the doorstep of other people's hopes and tragedies you cease to care. I wonder if she'd go on looking as bright as that if she knew something had gone wrong, or don't they tell her?"

Marda had been looking at that room and thinking those thoughts for nearly three hours, and with each minute that ticked by, fear took a further grip on her; it was as though it was holding her stomach with fingers made of icicles. She had been brought up not to show her feelings, to stick up her chin, and to face whatever was coming, but this deadly waiting was wearing to her courage. It was nearly three hours ago that she had heard the lift come down and the sound of a wheeled stretcher pushed up the corridor towards the operating theatre. What was Mannheim doing? Could it possibly take so long to lift whatever it was that was pressing on Jim's optic nerves, or had Jim collapsed under the anaesthetic? Was there even now a desperate effort being made in the operating-room with injections and artificial respiration? Was that what this long wait meant? Shirley under cover of the table looked at her watch for the hundredth time. She spoke in an elaborately cheerful voice.

"I'd say they wouldn't be long now."

Marda's heart raced so fast that it hurt, and her voice came in jerks.

"No; they ought to be out any minute."

The secretary bustled in with an armload of forced spring flowers, and her eye ran over Marda.

"This is a wretched long time that you've had to sit here. It's really better, you know, not to come to the nursing home, then you don't know exactly what time the operation starts, and only get the telephone call the moment it's over."

"Is she being nice, and speaking to us because she knows there's some bad news coming?" Marda wondered.

Shirley answered the secretary.

"Doctor Littlejohn says that Mr. Mannheim's a genius, but that he always works slowly."

"I believe he's considered a very clever man," the secretary agreed. "But we don't know much of his work here. He's usually in Switzerland, I believe."

Shirley eyed her sourly.

"Dumb ass," she thought. "Even if she knew Mannheim was a butcher who'd never done an operation in his life, can't she see that this is a fool time to say so?"

"I guess he's about the cleverest man living," she said loudly.

The secretary wrote down a name on a piece of paper and hurried towards the door. There she turned to Marda with a bright smile.

"You mustn't worry, you know. No news is good news."

Shirley watched the door close.

"It's a funny thing. Get yourself inside a hospital or a clinic and there doesn't seem one damn fool proverb they don't bring out. I'll take a bet with you that if you'd slipped down the steps and broken your leg when we brought Jimmie in, someone in this place would have said, 'It never rains but it pours.' Freddie says that you get like that. He finds himself making twenty clichés every day, but I guess that isn't right, for he's a most original talker."

Marda took a grip on herself, and managed something that looked like a smile. "You and your Freddie."

Shirley felt that any conversation, even a one-sided one, was better for Marda than silence.

"Funny I never thought I'd fall for a doctor." Marda's mind was not on what was being said.

"No?"

"But that day when Doctor Ewart came in with Freddie behind him I knew I'd got my ticket in the marriage lottery. I guess I'd been thinking that off and on since I was ten. I don't reckon I've ever seen a man since I was out of socks that I didn't kind of eye, in case he was the one I'd take by the arm and walk up a strip of red carpet, while the organ played 'The Voice that breathed o'er Eden.' Though, mind you, it was more than that about Jimmie. You know, I really was plumb crazy about him, for he certainly has got the charm and the looks. But I see now I made a mistake, and anyhow I never was a girl to fool around wasting my time, and it was as plain as the nose on your face where Jimmie's heart had got to. I guess that's what got me; it makes me mad as a hornet to see a man that's so crazy about another girl that he hasn't time for me. You know, even though I love Freddie, and I'll always think him the cream on my cup of tea, I guess that all my life through I'll be going crazy about some man or other. I told Freddie that, and he said he expected that would come natural to me, and I wouldn't be able to help myself; but as long as it was only a short attack, and I don't give way to it more than I need, he'll make do."

"Ssh!" said Marda, "was that a door opening?"

They listened a moment, then Shirley shook her head.

"A door, not the door." She opened her bag and took out a flask. "Brandy?" She poured some into the cup and passed it to Marda. "Drink that; it'll do you good."

Marda shook her head.

"No, thank you."

Shirley got up.

"You'll drink it if I have to pour it down your throat. Freddie gave it me. 'If we take more than three hours,' he said, 'have a nip, and give Marda a nip; you'll both need it.'" She giggled. "And drink it quickly; we don't want that female in the green coat coming in and finding us turning this morgue into a bar."

Marda swallowed the brandy, and it went warmly down to her nerve centres. She felt better. She gave a wobbly laugh.

"What luck Edward had laryngitis. If Vera were with us I don't think I could stand it, could you?"

Shirley gulped her brandy and pulled a fatuous face. "Nobody knows how terribly worried a poor little sister is at a time like this."

Marda smiled, but her voice was serious.

"I'll never understand her, I can't see how she comes to be Jim's sister. It seems so odd to go on coming to the house after behaving as she did. After all, she nearly talked Jim into not seeing Mannheim. How awful if she's right, if—"

Shirley broke in hurriedly.

"You never will understand her, so I wouldn't try. But I understand her. In a way, you know, you couldn't get a post-card between us two girls; we think plumb along the same lines. I know what tricks she's going to use before she ever opens her mouth, because I use the same tricks myself. The difference between us is that I don't fool myself about me, but Vera fools herself about herself. She doesn't know she's the world's biggest cad. She's kidded herself that she said all she did from the grandest motives, just as she's kidded herself that she always wanted you to marry Jimmie. Now it suits her to make up to you, for you'll be soft-hearted about Edward."

"I don't know that I will."

"Oh yes, you will." Shirley's voice was regretful. "I can see the scene as clearly right now as if it were being acted in front of me. You're in bed, and the new baby is in your arms. It's your first, and I guess it's a boy, half like you and half like Jimmie, and Jimmie's kneeling there looking first at his son, and then at you, not knowing which to eat first he's so crazy about both, and then you look up at him—it's a pity we can't have organ music here—and you say, 'But Jim, darling, we mustn't be selfish; we mustn't let little Edward suffer, because we've got a boy of our very own.'"

A door opened, steps were heard running. Marda got up, looking green and patchy.

"Listen."

Shirley put her arm round her.

"Come on. Take a grip on your guts."

Marda dug her nails into Shirley's arm, quite unconscious of what she was doing.

"Suppose he's died under the anaesthetic. I can't live without him—I can't."

Shirley's own heart was thumping, but she kept her voice casual.

"Don't act the fool. He's not going to die; he's going to see. There you are, it really is him this time. That's the wheels of the stretcher."

Holding their breaths the two girls clung together, listening to the approaching wheels. They heard the lift doors open, they heard the stretcher pushed in and the lift rising. There was quiet talking outside. Marda pulled away from Shirley, forced back her shoulders, and raised her chin. Freddie came in first, and held the door open for Mannheim. Mannheim had been so intent on his work that the world outside was shut off and he still had an aloof air. He came straight to Marda and took her hands, patting them but not speaking. Terrified, Marda stared at him; her lips opened twice before she could force out:

"How is he?"

Mannheim shook his head.

"One is human. I warned him I might be wrong, and if so there was nothing more that one could do."

"Nothing more!" Marda swayed. "Nothing more!" Her voice tailed away, and she sank in a faint at Mannheim's feet.

Marda came to herself almost as she touched the floor, and opened her eyes. For a moment or two she struggled to clear her blurred vision and to rid her ears of ringing bells; then she saw Mannheim, and remembrance swept back on her. She gave a moan, and at once he was kneeling beside her and holding her hands.

"What a big fool is this old doctor! Never for one instant did I think what you were fearing. But he is splendid, that man of yours. Why, I said to Doctor Freddie, 'He has the constitution of an ox, this one.'" Freddie nodded.

"Those were your very words."

Mannheim was still looking at Marda.

"My English it fails me after a big operation. When I am tired then my words slip. That is how I have told you things a little wrong."

Marda gripped his hand.

"Then what is it you're trying to say?"

Mannheim in his white coat looked more like St. Peter than usual. He sat on the floor, so as to bring himself on a level with Marda.

"There, that is better. When you came to see me, so that I might test Mr. Longford's eyes, I told you some things. I showed you pictures, and I explained to you, and to him, that it was possible all, or part, of his sight might be saved. When I came to operate I found conditions were not quite as I had planned. I found some little things that I could not foresee. There were for me two alternatives: one was to try an operation that I have always believed could be carried out, but I have never before had the opportunity to attempt; the other was to do nothing, and return him to his bed, blind as he was before. What should I do? The man is strong, he can stand an operation, even a dangerous operation. I have faith; it may be that I have made a great discovery. To do nothing is to condemn him to blindness for the rest of his life."

"And you operated!" said Marda, "and the operation was a failure. That's what you're trying to tell me, isn't it?"

"No, no, no." Mannheim shook his head. "You seem to me a young lady of great sense, and I am telling you everything. I have performed the operation. But I say I am human. I may be wrong. That I do not know what may be the outcome. I can only hope. It will be many weeks before we shall know. There must be rest, absolute rest in the darkness, so nature may perform her work."

Marda's fingers dug into Mannheim's hand.

"But there is hope?"

He took his time before he answered.

"Yes. I have made an experiment, you understand; but if what I have dreamed can happen have happened, then others will say I have work a miracle. For then Mr. Longford will see."

Marda got up.

"I'm sorry for being such a fool. When can I see him?"

"In a few days. You must be with him a great deal; you will help him. He has much to endure."

Shirley linked her arm in Marda's.

"Come on, then. I'll take you home."

Mannheim got up and dusted his knees.

"No. It is I who will take Miss Mayne home. As we are coming out of the operating-theatre Doctor Freddie confided in me that he is hoping to take you to lunch, Miss Shirley. There is no reason why that plan should be discomposed."

"Upset," suggested Freddie.

Mannheim laughed.

"He's always ready with the corrections, this doctor of yours, Miss Shirley. You must see to it that he does not bully you."

Shirley grinned.

"I'll say you don't know me. There's no more chance of that than of Marda bullying Jimmie."

Standing on the steps of the nursing home, waiting for Mannheim's car, Marda and Mannheim watched Shirley and Freddie drive off in a taxi.

"That young man has a great future," Mannheim said. "Do you think that little girl is the one to help him?"

The car drew up at the foot of the steps, and Marda got in.

"You can never tell. She's got all the gifts in the world if she likes to use them."

He smiled.

"English people are to me very funny. For you many things are desirable in a wife which to us are not so desirable. It is true that Miss Shirley has many good gifts, but are they those to make a good wife?"

"It depends what you want from your wife."

He looked at her.

"You have those gifts which in my country we think desirable."

"What?"

"In your Marriage Service it says, 'For richer, for poorer, in sickness and in health, to love, cherish, and to obey, till death us do part.' That I think you will truly say. For his own sake you wish that Mr. Longford could see, but for you it is all the same. You will cherish him whether he is blind, or whether he is not."

Marda was frankly surprised.

"Of course. You see I love him."

"Is that you, Marda?" said James.

She came across the darkened room and kissed him.

"Yes, darling, and I've got news for you at last. Mannheim is coming tomorrow to take off the bandages."

"Oh! I hadn't thought it would be before Monday." He stroked her hands. "I wonder how I'd have borne these weeks if there hadn't been any you. Bring up a chair, darling; I want to talk."

She drew a small armchair to the side of the bed.

"Well?"

He paused, feeling for his words.

"If Thursday is a complete washout I want to put off our marriage for a year."

Marda braced herself.

"I was expecting some rubbish of this sort. Is this Vera's idea or yours?"

He smiled.

"Vera's said something, of course; you can't expect the leopard to change his spots. She's messed about in my pie for so long that she can't let it go now. But as a matter of fact she said it'd be a good thing if we married at once, because if you were about it would save me having a nurse."

Marda laughed.

"She can be silly. Trying to work up a picture of me as the household drudge, I suppose." Then her voice grew serious. "All the same, though I know you don't take what she says seriously, it has had some effect, because since she saw you your night nurse reports that you've not been sleeping so well, and I have guessed that you were turning something over in your brain, so now lie still and listen to me without interrupting. You've been saying to yourself, 'Is it fair to let her marry me if the operation's a failure? Will she do it in pity? Ought she to have time to think it over?' Now hear what I've been doing. I've taken a little house down at Crockham Hill for us. I've signed the lease, and I've engaged the staff."

"But—"

"I told you not to interrupt. First of all, I've sacked Mrs. Barlow. I sacked her a week after your operation. I gave her a month's notice. As a matter of fact I weakened on that because she cried, and said she'd been in the house so long it was like her home, so I said she could stay on till we closed it. I can't think why she wants to stop, because she doesn't like Shirley and she hates me. When we get down to Crockham Hill, Daisy's going to be our cook temporarily. She's been taking cooking lessons ever since you were in the home."

"But—"

"Don't interrupt. Then I asked Tims to come with us as butler, and to look after you, and Mason to come as housemaid, but they hesitated rather. That was a shock. It was quite a time before I wormed out of them why, and then I found out that they're going to get married."

James forgot that he was arguing about plans and chuckled.

"Billy the Bowler did that for them."

"That's right, so they are coming to us as a married couple; but I don't see quite how you and I are going to live at Crockham Hill without being married. The country is very fussy about that sort of thing."

"Well, there's Shirley; a ward is a chaperone."

"Shirley's getting married just as soon as you can stand up to give her away. She's only left fixing the wedding day until you're up. She thought you'd better have the suspense about yourself off your mind first, because her wedding's going to cost such an awful lot, she thought the news might be bad for you. It's got to be at St. Margaret's, Westminster, with peals of bells, and red carpets, and, as a sop to Vera, Edward as a train-bearer."

James stretched out and found her hand.

"But, darling, none of this alters the feet that you must have time to think. It's all right now, we're very much in love. But let's suppose the worst. That I am not going to see again. What about the years ahead? Love of the sort we know now doesn't last, and affection and companionship take its place—at least they do in a normal match; but one half of what normal people do together may be cut off from us. Theatres, travel, all the little things of life."

Marda burst in.

"Theatres! Travel! How can you be such an idiot! As if those things mattered. The only thing that matters to me is that I shall spend the rest of my life with you. You forget that it was a blind man that I fell in love with, and if the worst should happen, and this operation be a failure, it's a blind man I shall go on loving." She made her voice light. "Besides, there's always the chance that I shan't be half as happy with you if you can see. You may go tearing over the countryside, playing games and all the rest of it. Besides, blindness can't take from us the things that really matter." He couldn't see that she flushed. "You know I said just now that Daisy is coming to us temporarily as a cook. It's temporary because what she wants is to be a Nanny. She's always wanted that, and I've promised her."

James pulled her to him.

"Put your head on the pillow beside me." He ran his hand over her face. "Is that what you want, Marda? Are you absolutely sure? It's so strange that you should care for me, a girl like you, with your looks and all, who could marry anyone they liked."

The door opened. Marda jumped to her feet. Mannheim, Freddie and the matron of the home stood in the doorway.

"I do not think," said Mannheim, "it is good to have things hanging over one's head. It makes for agitation. So when I tell Miss Mayne this morning that I will take off the bandages tomorrow, what I mean is I will take them off this afternoon."

James gripped the bedclothes.

"Today. Oh, but . . ."

Mannheim came over to the bed and laid his hand on his shoulder.

"It is a big day for you and a big day for me. It may be I have made, as you say in England, the bloomers . . ."

"Bloomer," said Freddie.

Mannheim looked hurt.

"How is that? Are there not two legs?"

The matron cleared her throat.

"Will you wait outside, Miss Mayne?"

"Please," said James, "let her stop."

Mannheim patted his shoulder.

"No. That is all arranged. Doctor Littlejohn has brought Miss Shirley. The two young ladies will wait together and drink tea. In England, all anxiety is allayed by the drinking of tea."

Marda and James could not kiss each other with the room full of people, so without a word Marda went into the passage. Shirley was waiting and drew her into the nurses' sitting-room.

"My! It's terrible the tea these nurses eat," she complained. "Buttered buns, scones and cakes; no girl could keep her figure in a place like this." She looked at Marda's white face, and pushed her into a chair.

"I don't want anything to eat, thank you," said Marda.

"I'll tell the world you don't," Shirley agreed, cheerfully, "but I've got what we need." She produced a brandy flask. "Just a little lacing of the tea. Nothing like it to keep the heart up."

"I can't drink brandy at four in the afternoon," Marda protested.

"You can and you'll like it." Shirley poured brandy into the two cups. "Now, there's no good fussing; I've got a lot of work for you to do. Just take a look at this." She passed over a list. "I want you to check it. I've got another in my pocket. It starts at the first column on that page. Twelve camiknicks, white satin. Twelve camiknicks, blue chiffon. Twelve coral camiknicks, chiffon with satin borders . . ."

Through eighteen pages, Shirley read her list of trousseau, then suddenly Marda laid down the papers and gave a gasp.

"Shirley, I've just thought of something. Just now, when Mannheim came in, Jim said, 'A girl like you with your looks and all could marry anyone they liked.' I didn't think, when he said it, what he meant, and anyhow there wasn't time to argue. If he gets his sight back he thinks I'm going to look like you described, and not at all like me."

Shirley put her list down on the tea table. For once she was winded.

"Jehoshaphat! That's tough." Then she looked at Marda with impatience. "Every day for two and a half months you have sat around holding that fellow's hand. What the hell do you talk about, anyway?"

"Well, not my looks; they haven't come into it."

"But you knew he might be going to see."

"Of course, but I'd forgotten all about what you said. It never seemed to crop up."

Shirley shook a despairing head.

"You dumb dames who don't give a damn how you look don't make any sense out of life. Now what are we going to do? Course you can send for me, and I can say it was a joke, but if the poor sap likes a blonde it's going to be pretty awful. Anyway, you can't do anything about it now. Either he sees you in ten minutes or he never sees you, so let's finish checking up this trousseau."

Twenty minutes later the door opened and Freddie came in.

"You can go in now, Marda." Marda thankfully dropped the twenty-fifth page of the list.

"How . . . ?"

Freddie shook his head.

"Send her in and tell her nothing, that was the old boy's orders."

Outside James' door, by the passage window, Mannheim was standing; his face was lifted to the sky. As Marda came to him she saw his eyes were full of tears. Pity for this old man who had tried so hard and failed flooded over her to the exclusion of thoughts for herself and James.

"Don't mind. You did all you could."

Mannheim's face was glowing as if he were thanking a power above his own for what had occurred. Tears of gratitude ran down his cheeks.

"Go to him," he said, gently; "he can see."

James was propped up in bed, the bandages were off his eyes. He was wearing dark glasses. Marda, forgetting all about herself and the shock her appearance must be to him, came to the foot of the bed.

James shook his head as he used to do in a sudden light.

"Is that you, Marda? I can't see very well yet. Everything is still blurred." He peered at her. "But you're not Marda."

She stood where she was, conscious now of the horrible deception that had been practised on him.

"Yes, I am. I'm sorry. Shirley told you I was pretty and fair, but it wasn't true. I . . ."

He held out a hand to her. She came and knelt by his bed.

"I'm so glad. I was knocked cockeyed when Shirley told me how you looked. Yours is the face that I had in my dreams. Shirley said you were fair and fluffy, but I could never see you that way."

"You don't mind?"

"Mind!" He drew her face towards his and whispered before he kissed her, "'Did never face so please my mind?'"

*

James and Marda were walking in the wood. James ran a frond of dead bracken through his fingers.

"One of the few good things that have come out of being blind is the new pleasure you get from each season of the year. I wonder if I shall go on feeling that."

Marda looked round at the yellowing leaves.

"You'll soon have a chance to find out. It's autumn again, and you saw the winter last year."

"Not very well. I still had to wear my black glasses. Things were misty right on into the spring."

She smiled.

"Yes, the only time you had the black glasses off was for Shirley's wedding."

He made a face.

"I've never been so scared. I thought I was certain to fall over something, and I can't imagine anything worse than making an ass of myself at Shirley's wedding."

She stopped.

"Fancy, in another month we shall have been married a year."

He turned her round to face the other way.

"Come on, you've walked far enough. I promised Nurse I wouldn't let you get tired."

"I'm not tired."

He drew her back towards the house.

"No, but you will be with all your family coming, not to mention Shirley; it's a big day."

There was a back gate from their garden leading into the wood, and at it stood Tims.

"What is it, Tims?" Marda called out.

"It's Doctor Mannheim, Madam."

Her face lit up; she turned to James.

"Oh, good! The old angel's made it. I was so afraid he wouldn't." She looked after Tims, who was hurrying back through the garden to the house. "Of course, you never saw Tims as he used to be in Thurloe Square, but I don't believe, if I met him now as he used to be then, that I'd recognise him. He's quite pink, and he's really a different shape."

James laughed.

"Do you think that's the country air, or Ada?"

"Both. Ada told me the other day that she didn't know it was possible to be so happy. It made me feel quite a beast to hear her say it, because it's a funny kind of married life they have really. They've only got a bedroom that they can call their own, for there's always cook and the kitchen maid in their sitting-room, and sometimes Daisy."

James paused to let his eye take in the gay berries on a hedge.

"Happiness has nothing to do with space. I should love you just as much in one room."

Mannheim was waiting in the drawing-room. He came across and took Marda's hand.

"Every day since your so beautiful letter came, I have said to myself, How shall I get to England? How can I arrange it so there will be no patients to disturb me when I want to come?"

"And how did you arrange it?" Marda asked.

Mannheim's eyes twinkled.

"To everybody I said, 'You must not have that operation in the autumn; that is not a good time. Winter perhaps, summer perhaps, but never in the autumn.'" He turned to James. "I hear good accounts of you, my friend. Doctor Freddie he writes to me regularly."

"He sees me regularly," James agreed. "I know it's just his way of earning enough money to keep Shirley, so I let him pretend that it's because he wants to look at my eyes."

"And now," said Mannheim, looking round, "where is mademoiselle?"

"She'll be down soon."

"And she is, I suppose, quite different to all other babies. She knows you and smiles at you."

"As a matter of fact," said Marda, "she is rather exceptional. If she hadn't been I shouldn't have asked you to come all the way from Switzerland to be her godfather." There was the sound of a car outside, and she went to the door. "That sounds like the family. It's too noisy a car for Freddie's and Shirley's handsome beast."

All the Mayne family, and Hannah, were packed into the car outside. Clarice was out first. She had Belisha under her arm. He had a silver bow on his collar.

"Look, Marda, he's got a bow on for the christening. I thought it ought to be white satin, but Hannah said that was only for weddings."

Hannah was looking very grand in a plum-coloured overcoat, and a plum-coloured felt hat with green leaves on it.

"My goodness, Hannah," said Marda admiringly, "you look very posh."

Hannah got out of the car, and gave her coat a satisfied pat.

"'Tisn't often I'm rigged out all new, Miss Marda dear, but I said to myself, 'You shall be this time; you won't be godmother to Miss Marda's baby more than once in your lifetime.'"

"She's new underneath, too," said Edward.

Hannah flushed.

"Give over, Master Edward. That's not at all a nice way to talk, and you don't know nothing about it."

Edward gave Marda a brotherly hug.

"Don't I just, with you machining at yards of pink stuff with yellow daisies on it."

Alice kissed Marda.

"How are you, darling, and how's baby?"

Alistair held his daughter by the shoulders and looked at her.

"Not too bad. Still a little bit on the thin side. Not doing too much, are you?"

Marda put an arm through each of her parents'.

"No, you old fusspot. Come in and see Doctor Mannheim."

"Can I see baby?" asked Alice.

"She'll be down in a minute. The christening's in half an hour."

"Oh, there's Shirley and Freddie," said Clarice. "Gosh, look at Shirley's hat!"

Marriage had improved Shirley. She was more beautiful than ever. She had a serenity that had been missing before. She flung herself on Marda.

"How are you? I guess the baby's looking just darling. I've got a present for her here. I was afraid we'd be late; Freddie would drive so slowly."

"Slowly!" Marda looked at Freddie. "Doesn't sound like you."

"Can't be too careful," said Freddie.

Marda turned ecstatically to Shirley.

"Are you—?"

Shirley nodded.

"That's right. April, and I certainly am pleased."

It was Daisy who brought the baby down to the drawing-room, a quite transformed Daisy. She had done a course at a training college, and felt herself the most experienced nurse. She was proud of her grey coat and skirt and black hat, the badges of a first-class nanny. Marda took the baby from her, and sat down, and laid her on her knee, where everybody could see her.

"May I introduce you all? This is Miss Felicity Alice Longford."

Felicity gave a little yawn and opened speedwell-blue eyes and looked round. Mannheim felt in his pocket and brought out a string of coral beads. Shirley opened a jewel box and pinned a brooch, with Felicity written in diamonds, on to the bib. Hannah turned rather pink.

"I've got something for her here, Miss Marda, but it can keep."

"Come on, Hannah, don't be shy; it's a lovely present," said Clarice.

Hannah thus urged shoved a leather box into Marda's hand. Inside was a spoon and fork.

"Something to eat with," she explained. "You see, it comes natural to me to think of food, Miss Marda dear."

There was a cough in the doorway, and Tims came forward.

"There's a little something for Miss Felicity, from me and Mrs. Tims."

James gave him a smile.

"Well, fetch Ada in."

Ada was only just outside the door; she had a parcel in her hand. Tims cleared his throat.

"We thought we'd give her something so she starts as she means to go on, sir."

Ada put the parcel into James' hand. He unwrapped the tissue paper and produced a moneybox with a greyhound on the top.

"By Jove! Billy the Bowler!"

"Though it was Ada who won," said Shirley. "Don't you remember? Billy the Bowler never ran."

"But he did later, Madam," Tims protested, "and did us very well."

Marda looked up.

"On behalf of Felicity, thank you all very much for her lovely presents." She stroked Felicity's frock. "She's wearing your frock, Mums, and your petticoat, Clarice; she's got the duck you sent swimming in her bath, Edward, and she brushes her hair with your brush, Dad. In fact she's been very well treated by everybody except her mother and father, and they haven't given her anything at all."

Alice smiled at Alistair.

"D'you remember Marda's christening? I said just the same thing."

Alistair smiled back at her.

"And I said, that if you'd given her something of yourself she wouldn't need any other present."

James nodded.

"That's how I feel. If there's even a little of Marda in Felicity she doesn't need the good fairies at her christening, for she has the best gifts already."

THE END

FURROWED MIDDLEBROW

*titles available in paperback only

**pseudonym of Noel Streatfeild